by
Amber Jameson

SILVER MINK BOOKS
An Imprint of Silver Moon

PO Box CR25 Leeds LS7 3TN
and
PO Box 1614 New York NY 10156

New authors welcome

Printed and bound in Great Britain

SILVER MINK is an imprint of SILVER MOON BOOKS
of LEEDS

[Silver Moon Books of Leeds and Silver Moon Books of London are in no way connected]

If you like one of our books you will probably like them all!
To order other titles see details and extracts on back pages

For free 20 page booklet of extracts from previous books (and, if you wish to be on our confidential mailing list, from forthcoming monthly titles as they are published) please write to:-
    Silver Moon Reader Services

PO Box CR 25 LEEDS LS7 3TN
or
PO Box 1614 NEW YORK NY 10156

Surely the most erotic freebie ever!!

THE CAPTIVE first published 1995
Copyright Amber Jameson

THE CAPTIVE

This is fiction - in real life, practice safe sex

CHAPTER ONE

Laughter, musical and happy, drifted across the castle garden. The girl was as beautiful as her laughter, a rare beauty that came from within.

Her gown was of fine thin silk, a simple shift, caught below the breasts by a narrow thong of gold. He could see through it the shape of her long legs. And oh those breasts! His mouth watered as he gazed at them bouncing freely under the unrestricting silk.

He was still sweating hard from his fencing lesson as he stood taking his breath, leaning against the castle gallows. The exercise had made his blood flow fast at the sight of her and the badge of his masculinity was rising painfully beneath his short leather practice tunic.

Her name was Zacora. He had noticed her before, and enquired.

His father promised him that as soon as he had taken part in his first joust he could choose a girl as his wife. Could he wait that long? No! The fencing master had told him there was much work to do before he was ready for a tournament.

Still his desire grew. It was too much. Clenching his fists, Ogham howled, howled aloud like an animal.

There was a sudden silence on the castle lawn and and then Zacora came running. The very sight of her approaching him was an aphrodisiac and the pain in his groin was unbearable.

"Are you ill?" Her voice was like music; each word stroked his belly and caressed his penis.

"Not now!"

The two young people stood together in the menacing shadow of the gallows. Zacora lowered her sapphire blue eyes and folded her hands at the top of her thighs, just as she had been taught to do in her lessons in womanhood.

Breathing was difficult for Ogham. The girl's sex was clearly outlined by her white silk dress and the way her hands lay at that very point.

"What have you learned today?" he asked, taking in the creamy bare skin of her arms and imagining what they would look like bound to the gallows. And those long legs coiled around the post to open her up. He had to close his eyes, screw them tight, he could not bear to see her, the thoughts of that luscious body bound and at his mercy were too much.

She stretched out a hand to stroke his chin, still smooth with youth. Her obvious concern made Ogham hide a smile. This was going to be easy.

He gave a brave grin, shaking his head. "You haven't told me what you learned."

"Oh, how to kiss a man's penis with the vagina." She related it so matter-of-factly and yet her eyes were still lowered modestly.

Ogham's throat seemed to be closing with desire, but this girl wasn't what his father would choose for him. Or allow him to choose. Rumour had it that although her father was a nobleman, her mother was a mere chambermaid. It was her beauty which brought her to court and the classes for the young ladies.

"Anything else?" he asked.

Zacora shook her head, her long golden hair waving like spun silk and catching the sun to throw out silver highlights. "There wasn't time." Although her head was still bowed with submissiveness, there was laughter in her voice and he could see her eyes twinkling.

"But you've been in there all morning!"

"I know, but one of the girls was disobedient."

She looked up at him. Her wide soft lips were parted and he could see even white teeth and the pinkness of a tongue tip. He could imagine all of these engulfing his painfully hard penis. She seemed to be inviting him to place his whole length in her mouth.

"What did this girl do? This disobedient one?" It was difficult for him to speak, so great was his need. He was ready for a woman, must have one, no matter what his father said.

Zacora lifted her dress, unveiling the creamy length of her athletic legs right up to the silver triangle of hair, for she was naked beneath. Ogham held his breath. "The girl pleasured herself," she said gravely, pouting her sex and opening it by pulling at the firm young lips.

He could see everything! The pink folds, shining in the sunshine and the hardened bud of her clitoris. The folds shone with moisture and even with his limited experience of women, Ogham knew what that meant. She was ready for him.

"Was she punished?" His hands were sweating and his body glowed with need. He had the fire of a man in him.

"Indeed she was," said Zacora. "It was Peeka. There she is. She got her bottom smacked very thoroughly."

Ogham followed the direction of the delicate pointing finger and saw another fair girl, pretty but not as beautiful as Zacora. She seemed none the worse for wear. He held out his hand. "Let's go into the forest and you can tell me all about it." Keeping his voice light and carefree was a problem, but he managed it.

The folds of fine gossamer silk were allowed to fall, hiding the sex treasures once more, and Zacora lowered her eyes. "I can tell you here," she said meekly. "I do not wish to disobey you, but no girl goes into the forest."

"Unless she is betrothed?" That was what she would be thinking. He grabbed her hand, holding it cruelly, squeezing her fingers.

She nodded. "Unless they are betrothed." Her golden head was still lowered, but his touch, though painful, stimulated her. Her body was flushed and a lethargic heaviness lay in the nakedness of her belly.

"I like you," he stammered. "I like you very much."

Did that mean they would be betrothed? Zacora looked up at him shyly, that same inviting smile on her lips. Soon he would be a knight, riding into battle and leaving his wife behind, safe in her chastity belt. Perhaps he would indeed ask her to be his wife if she encouraged him. Just a little!

"Perhaps we could go a little way," she said. "Just into the edge of the forest." She wanted to so much. Hesitantly, reluctantly, but driven by desire she could not control, she began to walk with him across the lawns to the thickly wooded wilderness beyond the castle grounds.

"Tell me about Peeka." In the green light of the forest, ever changing as the breeze moved the abundant leaf canopy, his voice was steadier. "Tell me how she was punished." He knew it would be punishment for himself to listen. The story would increase the pain in his organ until he could bear it no longer.

She took a deep breath. Talking about another girl was better than worrying about herself, worrying lest she be seen in the forest with a man to whom she was not betrothed. "It happened when the Master was describing how a woman should ripple her vagina along the length of a man's cock."

There was no trace of embarrassment in her voice as she told the tale, but then a woman's whole life was devoted to giving a man pleasure.

"Peeka lifted her dress and used one of the Master's pleasure tools inside herself, before she was given permission."

"Very disobedient!" Ogham pressed Zacora's willowy figure to him, feeling the sweep of her hips and the jut of her buttocks, and she hardly resisted at all.

"The Master was furious!" Now Zacora nestled against the strength of Ogham's young body. "The stupid ignorant girl had taken her own virginity, you see, there in the class. We are taught to wait until it is taken from us in whichever way our man requires."

"Of course." Ogham swayed against her. His legs had lost their strength. "So she was whipped?"

Zacora nodded. "She was placed in the stocks, completely naked, and we were all made to watch or help." She turned to him with wide innocent eyes, eyes which made him feel that he was drowning in his own sexual need. "Each wrist and her neck were clamped in the heavy wood of the stock, while her back and bottom were pressed out ready for the birching."

"And her legs, were they free?" With one hand slipped securely round Zacora's waist, he let the other stray to her breasts, one after the other. The nipples sprang to hard little pips under the silk. She was so receptive, he thought. She learned her lessons with the Master well.

"No!" she exclaimed. "They were shackled and spread well apart and the Master made Peeka keep the training phallus in her vagina."

"Was there any sign of humiliation?"

"She didn't cry," Zacora told him, "in fact, she pouted her quite plump buttocks high."

"She was ready, then?"

Ogham's male sword, cramped in his tight breeches, squirmed against the restriction of the leather. With Zacora nestling under his strong arm the thought of Peeka almost asking to be birched, plump and naked, was too much.

"Hm," agreed Zacora, cuddling closer. "Very ready, The Master showed us how her juices trickled copiously down the phallus and even..." She paused, looking up at him, her eyes wide and her lips moistly parted. "Even down her thighs."

A sigh, long and painful, whispered along the path which they were treading. Ogham had never had a woman although his father had told him what it was like to sink into the joyous welcome of female parts. All women in Lokara were taught how to pleasure a man to the full.

"Describe Peeka's bottom," he begged.

Zacora stopped, resting against the massive trunk of an ancient oak. She closed her eyes, not seeing Ogham rub his painfully erect shaft. "Her bottom was spread wide by the shackles." She traced her hands to the shape of well opened buttocks and widely splayed legs. Her long fingers also traced a vertical line to denote the deep cleft. The fingers stroked away from her body, depicting the voluptuous curves of each buttock cheek. "We could all see her rose hole and it was pulsing madly. The flesh of her bottom cheeks quivered, The Master says that plump buttocks always quake more than slim ones when they are waiting for a blow to fall."

Ogham's green eyes were wide as he stared at Zacora's beauty. She was describing the scene so vividly that he felt that he was in the training room with them. He approached her tentatively, looking at her fairy-like beauty hidden only by a single layer of gossamer-fine silk.

"The Master took the training phallus from Peeka," Zacora continued. "It was then that she started to cry. She said she felt deprived without it. The Master laughed at her and, almost immediately, rammed the most monumental phallus into her, the type given to men as a betrothal present, up into Peeka's vagina, so she was on tip-toe."

The young squire placed his hands against the trunk of the oak, pressing the heat of his body against the girl. "Describe Peeka's cunt," he grated crudely.

The coarse word didn't offend Zacora, it excited her. Her golden head, with the mass of curls tumbling over her shoulders, leaned back against the tree. Her unfettered breasts felt full and swollen and the nipples pressed hard against the thin silk, hot and inflamed. Her mound felt more puffy than usual, pouting out towards this handsome squire. Surely this was what all her training was for; to please a man such as this, to snare him in her charms?

"Peeka was standing on tip-toe in the stocks to display her bottom and sex pouch properly, that's what we've been taught, you see, all our lives, to make ourselves pretty and subservient to men."

Ogham nodded. Quite right too!

"In the centre of Peeka's folds was the thickness of the training phallus, opening her vagina to the full. Her clitoris was juddering and was so swollen and scarlet I thought it was going to burst. The folds were swollen too and fluttering like butterfly wings. It was then that the Master struck the first blow."

"Does Peeka have a very pale skin?" Ogham was leaning the whole length of his body on Zacora's and squeezing the pliancy of her breasts.

"Oh, very," she nodded. Her nipples were being pinched cruelly and the breast flesh was kneaded like dough. It was her duty, she knew, to bear whatever pleased a man. "Much paler than mine. Her skin is almost white, whereas mine is creamy."

Ogham was lifting the silk which swathed Zacora's slender but curvaceous bottom. "What colour did her flesh become after the blows?"

"The first blow of the birch made a single scarlet stripe. Peeka flinched, but simply pressed her bottom out further for more." Zacora allowed the young squire to spread her own cheeks wide, his fingers digging painfully into the most delicate flesh of her rear valley. "She couldn't move very much because the stocks limit any wriggling."

"Have you ever been in them?" The delight of visualising the gorgeous Zacora naked in the stocks was unbearable.

She lowered her eyes, thick honey-blonde lashes sweeping her cheeks. "By the time the Master had finished there were ten very red weals across Peeka's pale skin, each exactly parallel with the other and mostly gathered across the plumpest part, where the cheeks curve down. At least two were striped across Peeka's sex lips."

"Stop!" ordered Ogham. "You haven't answered my question." He could feel a sheen of sweat beading his face. "Have you ever been in the stocks?"

Zacora's long thighs were open as he pressed his taut young body to hers. All her training had prepared her for this day and she wanted to enjoy it to the full, but there was still a small nagging doubt in her mind. Did he really like her as he said? She should not be behaving like this with a man to whom she was not betrothed, but surely...

"The stocks!" he hissed. "Wouldn't you like to experience what Peeka experienced?"

His strong young fingers were spreading her open, her buttocks, her sex lips. She knew he could feel her sex sap trickling warmly from the folds, soaking her clitoris which was pressing against his questing finger tips. Her will was gone. He sighed, grasping her hand. "Come on!" he growled hurriedly. "There won't be anyone in the training room now!"

It was early afternoon and most of the court was resting. There were a few guards on duty, but none stopped the two young people as they returned to the castle and entered the empty echoing training room. The stocks stood ready, sombre dark wood stained with old blood in places, the carefully placed holes for neck and wrists beckoning Zacora. She shuddered at the sight of them. The equipment seemed to be much more threatening when the other girls weren't there.

"Strip!" ordered Ogham. His voice was very commanding for so young a squire. "Strip for me! Is it not what you are taught to do?"

It was. But...

"Now!" he said again, even more sternly this time.

Obediently, as she had been taught, Zacora gathered the fine silk in her hands and lifted the hem, feeling very vulnerable without the film of gossamer swirling around her body. She bowed her head and folded her hands at the silver fronded crotch. She wasn't ashamed of her body, standing there naked didn't humiliate her, for she had been born to please her masters, the nobles of the kingdom.

Green eyes glittering, Ogham watched every move, every sway of her young limbs, the sheen of moisture on the neatly trimmed bush of silvery blonde hair at the top of her thighs.

"Let me see you in the stocks!"

Now she hardly hesitated. With long easy steps she made her way to the sombre punishment implement. "This is just a game? It must be a game we are playing. You won't lock me in, will you?"

Ogham said nothing, but helped the young maiden to place her slender neck on the curved block and place her wrists in the slots. The solid sound of wood on wood as he brought down the top half of the fiercesome contraption, made his penis swell yet more. He hesitated, wondering whether to slip the hasps of the padlocks, but the hesitation was only momentary. In a second it was done. The girl was caught fast.

At each end of the room there were windows, long and dusty. The grime made them act as mirrors and Zacora could see her naked backside lifted in the air. Ogham was shackling her ankles in the floor manacles so her legs were splayed, revealing her sex slit to the full. Unlike Peeka there was no need to stand on tip-toe, for Zacora's legs were long, she simply hollowed her back, posing her sex upwards.

"What shall I beat you with?"

"You must not beat me. I said it must be a game!"

He was standing behind her, his hands resting lightly on her buttock cheeks, his thumbs pressing the puffy lower edges of her sex lips.

She had no idea whether he was clothed or naked for he was bending low, examining her minutely. In that position she could not see him reflected in the grimy windows, but she knew that he could see every detail of her sex folds. What he was doing was no lover's caress and, for the first time, she felt shamed and humiliated.

He felt her tension and released his tight grip. "Are you going to scream?"

She shook her head, swaying the silky tresses from side to side. It would do no good to scream. There was no one within sound of them. And if there were, she would just be found with a man to whom she was not betrothed. She would be disgraced. Better not to be rescued. She had fallen into a trap and must make the best of it.

A laugh, cold and without mirth, rasped in her ears. "I think, just in case, we'll use the tongue bar." She heard him move across the room and then the chink of metal as he sorted through the Master's equipment. Returning to her, he held the device for her to see. She swallowed hard. It was a painful contraption.

A bar of iron with balls at each end was placed in the victim's mouth, depressing the tongue and held in place by a leather strap around the head. As he tightened the buckle, pulling it unmercifully, so that her head was shaken from one side to the other, he was breathing hard.

He moved to stand in front of her. A hot bulge was close to her helpless face. She could feel his penis throbbing like a caged wild animal.

"Yes!" he said. "Excellent!"

Zacora would have protested if it was possible, but her soft lips were fixed by the iron gag. There was no escape, she realised. She was trapped, completely trapped, but this sense of total helplessness gave that wonderful feeling of lethargy. Her eyes felt heavy. There was a liquid whirling in her belly; a melting heat. Her sap, as she was warned would happen when the time was right, was drooling down her pale thighs, hot and sticky.

Before that day in the beauty of the Lokara springtime, she never realised that being vulnerable could make her aware of her powerful sexuality.

Ogham held the polished wooden phallus before her eyes. Her sapphire orbs widened with fear. He wouldn't use that, surely! She was a virgin and must remain so until her betrothal.

Straining her neck she looked up into his deep green eyes. They glittered with cruelty in a face lightly tanned by days spent practising on the tournament field. His leather tunic lay discarded on the wooden floor and his lithe young chest was bare, heaving as he stood over her. Hooking his thumbs into the waistband of his breeches, he slid them down over his hips and thighs. Zacora could not gasp for the device clamped in her mouth would not allow any sound to issue from her mouth.

After giving her a glimpse of the monstrous swaying penis he disappeared from view. An image of it remained in her mind. Darker than his body skin, but still a pale flesh colour, it shone as if the skin was stretched to the limit. At the end was the globe, a perfect rounded cone, glistening with a sheen of its own dew. Below it hung the sac, full and taut, the two hard balls neatly drawn high between his muscular thighs.

She felt his hand smoothing over the firm curves of her bottom. He investigated their texture by pressing the two perfect hemispheres together and then parting them so that he could see every crease of the tight rose hole.

"Such perfect globes," he murmured, "should be warmed by the birch or the paddle. Which do you prefer? But, of course, you cannot speak." He gave a light laugh and showed her the two implements he had chosen; one in the left hand and one in the right. In his right hand was the birch and in his left was a broad bladed paddle.

It was difficult to believe that only that morning Zacora had watched plump Peeka's buttocks quiver and redden under the swish of the birch. She had watched two narrow welts appear from one broad buttock, across the plump and tender sex lips, to the other buttock cheek. It was almost possible to feel the pain for the girl, but Zacora longed for the excitement which Peeka obviously felt. The memory of the trailing silvery sex sap running from the newly broken gateway was a clear picture in her mind.

"Choose!" he insisted.

Zacora nodded to the left, to the paddle.

Ogham grinned broadly, slicing the chosen implement through the air and then slapping it across his own palm. He gave a grimace at the stinging pain and she hung her head, wishing that the game had never started.

He walked behind her, his paces slow and measured. She felt him smooth the paddle over her poised buttock mounds, measuring the stroke. As her excitement increased, her breasts became tauter, serving to heighten her excitement. She felt her open sex folds swell, making them more vulnerable and more clearly revealed. The humiliation began in earnest.

"You have no right to be at court, you dirty little bitch!"

Surely he had not said that! Then the paddle fell, swiping across the full bottom mounds. The sound of the thinly sliced wood hitting flesh was loud and echoed through the empty school room.

"You are not nobility!" The paddle slapped again, giving a burning stinging pain, overlapping the last.

I was invited to court, she wanted to say, but the iron gag prevented any sound. And I am nobility. You have no right to say that I am not.

Again the paddle slapped. Her firm, well-lifted bottom was on fire, but below that, her sex pouch was heating and melting. The juices were flowing from virginal folds.

"I'm going to fuck you." The words were rasped cruelly and smacked her ears like a blow from the paddle, but at the same time they were as stimulating.

The paddle slapped lightly at the soft, pouting sex folds. The blow wasn't hard enough to hurt, but it was more shaming than any given previously. It caused a squelching sound as the thin piece of wood pressed the liquids gathered between the inflamed leaves.

The paddle slapped down viciously on the uplifted buttocks, so beautifully rounded, sliding down at the end of the stroke to the open folds which dripped with her fluids. The continued discipline coloured them, Zacora knew that. It gave them a rosy glow where once they had been creamily pale. The punishment made her hot inside as well; the beautiful melting heaviness opened her up yet further.

The strokes of the paddle seemed unending. Her bottom flesh was a rounded fire, but the moist crease between them was hotter. Swollen folds created to take a man's sex sword. She wriggled, hollowing her back to present her moist silky entrance with the puffy silvery fronds at the best angle for him.

His breathing was harsh and quick. She knew that he was standing behind her, gazing at the scarlet welts which merged into two burning, swollen mounds. There was pain as he grasped the punished flesh to open it yet further. His thumbs spread the puffy lips, smearing the dew on the silver curls as he opened them fully. A flush suffused her face as she realised that he could see everything; every fold, every crease, every drop of sap and, in the centre, her swollen bud, pert and jerking.

Zacora wanted him to touch that, but he ignored it and she felt tears of frustration well in her moist eyes. But she knew that she must please him first. Her own pleasure was in what he gave her by bonding her in the stocks, making her feel vulnerable and by making her bottom glow.

There was a pressure at the silky entrance, a growing pressure, Zacora felt her eyes widen as she looked up at the vague reflection in the grimy window. Ogham was standing behind her, bracing himself on the heated mounds of her bottom and pressing himself against her.

At first the pressure was pleasant. It was a meeting of moist flesh, her own and his. She was helpless. She had no control over what he did to her. The pressure increased, pushing into her pitilessly. She could feel her vagina gateway being pushed open.

With a final thrust he was inside her. She heard him sigh pleasurably. The pain was a mere pinprick compared with the fire he had created in her helpless bottom.

For a brief moment he was still, as if he wasn't sure what to do next. The young squires were taught to fence and joust, but the sexual pleasing was left to the ladies of the court.

Knowing her duty, she gyrated her heated and punished flesh against the coolness of his groin. Her well-trained vaginal muscles caressed the thick length of his cock. She heard Ogham groan and he began to quicken his movements. Her flesh drew on his, pulling his penetrating shaft into her wet cushiony pillow.

A squire so young and inexperienced could not take a long caress. It had been hard for him to contain his seed in all the long moments of stimulating punishment.

Zacora felt her painfully confined breasts swell as she recognised his growing need to let go. His pumping was frantic; his vigorous young balls bounced rhythmically on her lifted and open sex lips. His organ seemed to be pulsating against every part of her nether regions. His seed emptied into her helpless body in a great rush of fluid heat. She offered him her opening, taking the torrent as it filled her. The young squire gave several more jerks into her, making sure that every drop drenched her newly opened pouch.

At last he pulled out of her, leaving her frustrated. Her own pleasure did not quite reach the peak, although her bud had throbbed close to it.

"You will be disgraced," he rasped.

She knew it was true but, muted, by the iron gag, she was unable to reply. Why, her mind cried. Why had he abused her so?

"My father will send you from the court." He laughed, the sound shrill with contempt. He wiped the end of his drooling globe across the burning mounds of her buttocks. "Perhaps I shall suggest that you should be strung on the gallows, naked with your legs splayed for all to see how you have been despoiled."

Ogham moved to allow her to see him. His penis, although so recently emptied, was partially erect and slick from the mixture of their juices. Slowly, he released the leather strap which held the iron gag between her lips.

Relieved, she glossed her lips with her tongue. "Peeka wasn't treated so cruelly," she whispered. Her mouth felt dry and her voice was hoarse through the long confinement with the gag.

"Peeka is a nobleman's daughter." he sneered.

"So am I."

"Not legitimately." He posed his sperm soaked globe at her mouth, pressing it between the soft lips. She could taste the salt, and such was her training, her tongue wrapped around it automatically in a moist caress.

"You'll be auctioned," he told her, pressing his length into her mouth. She took it as she had been taught, using the smooth, unresilient phalli. This was warm, pulsing and growing thicker as she sucked upon the living, throbbing length.

As she sucked obediently upon the young master's flesh, she thought how unfair it was that she should be humiliated in such a way. She saw herself on the gallows, her arms outstretched and tied at the wrists. Her breasts would be taut, but the nipples erect on the flattened flesh. The occupants of the castle, including the guards, would be at liberty to look up at her splayed legs and would see each moist fold.

"My father will delight in leaving you on the gallows until the auction," he sneered.

Miserably, she sucked his hard length. Her duty was to pleasure the man, no matter what imagined wrong he may have done.

In the land of Lokara a man could do no wrong. Zacora had been taught that from childhood.

CHAPTER TWO

It was auction day in the neighbouring land of Vakir and there was a churning sensation in Harold Meleagan's belly. Something wonderful was going to happen. He felt it in his organs, especially his male organs.

From the very moment he woke he knew that this would be a special day and when he saw the imported girl on the podium he knew that his gut feeling was right.

She was introduced as Zacora. Taller than the other girls; graceful, willowy, but full blown. Aristocratic. She was just what he needed to be his consort. She would compliment his accumulated wealth exactly.

It was the hair which caught his attention first. Among all the dark-skinned beauties, the pale skin, sapphire blue eyes and the golden hair streaked with silver made his blood run hot. The same hair, lightly curled, grew lushly from the pouting mound of her sex and tickled the tops of her perfect thighs. Yes, mused Harold, the sex hair was lush but neat, no beard to tangle with a man's enthusiasm. He adjusted his organ which was rearing mightily beneath his silken robes.

"This one says she is of noble birth," claimed the slave master.

Harold gave a quiet smile of triumph, knowing that his feeling had been correct, but there was crude laughter, a sound of disbelief, from the crowd of potential buyers. They were a mixed bunch. Some of the poorer ones just came to look, for the slave auction was always an entertainment. This was especially so when the girls destined to be sexual playthings were put upon the platform. They were always naked and always fearful. Some of them wept and pleaded to be allowed freedom.

His eyes remained fixed on the girl called Zacora. There was something about her. She was very special. It seemed that she had all the knowledge of every nuance of sexuality and yet she had the innocence of a cherub. He hugged himself, determined that she would be his; his consort to sit beside him on the... no, he chided himself, he must not think that far ahead.

He peered from his carriage at the crowd. They were rowdy that day. Mostly they were peasants come to town for the market, which was held on the same day as the auction. They were dressed in rough tunics, men and women alike, short and hardly decent. Their legs were bare apart from thongs of leather criss-crossing the flesh to hold the plates of rough hide to their feet. Baskets of produce were held on their hips or balanced on their heads. This method of transport of their wares hoisted their crude clothing yet higher, leaving their unfettered genitals free in the morning air. Such nudity encouraged sexual freedom and it wasn't unusual to see a couple take advantage for a quick release of their pleasure on the cobbles of the square amidst the debris of the market.

Harold shuddered at the crudity of it all. His companion, Megan, his Aunt, clearly revelled in it. Sometimes he wondered how she could be an Aunt of his. A strange woman, Megan, enjoying anything which smacked of the lower orders.

Amidst the mixed crowd there were some merchants, men like Harold, but he liked to think that he had risen above them. Their women hung on their arms. Wives were left at home and these pretty creatures were playthings, bought at previous auctions.

As they waited for the auction to begin the merchants took the opportunity to squeeze the breasts of this particular girl, beautifully highlighted by the flowing robes of rich silk. Others were bolder, folding the fine material until it was draped over the soft curve of the belly and it fell in delicate pleats like curtains framing the lushness of a sex bush they would delight in fingering.

Some of the other women displayed showed embarrassment or humiliation at such inspections by potential buyers, others were delighted. The latter would arch their back to give the merchant full access to the moistness of her sex. She would smile, urging him to bring her to orgasm.

Around the outside of the square there were carriages, carrying nobles, rich merchants like the Meleagans, and minor Princes from neighbouring lands. Harold saw one of these watching eagerly as the golden haired beauty was fondled and groped by the slave master. Harold smiled, slotting his eyes. The Prince of Vakir! The weakling was fast losing control of his life and his land.

The Prince stared unblinkingly as the slave master lifted up each full breast, cupping it and stroking the nipple.

The girl, Zacora, showed no sign of humiliation. She looked proud as her breasts were fondled in such an intimate manner, as though it was the slave master's right to treat her thus. Harold nodded approvingly at the girl's demeanour.

"She takes pain well, ladies and gentlemen," said the slave master. He held up a toothed device which flashed silver in the morning sunlight. Carefully, this was placed over one pink nipple. The man, smiling at his audience, let go and there was an audible click.

The blonde slave arched her willowy body backwards and the crowd made a whispered sound of appreciation. It seemed that the arch was not a distortion caused by pain, but to show her new adornment to the best advantage. The crowd saw the silver nipple clamp pinching the delicate skin into the toothed circle. The slave said nothing, but her wide, soft lips curved to a slight demure smile.

The crowd murmured their appreciation of the girl's conduct as the other breast was treated in the same manner.

"These devices," said the slave master, "although causing slight pain, do not mark the flesh, so there is no detraction in the value of your potential property, ladies and gentlemen." As he gave the clamps extra twists Zacora remained still, subservient and passive, but oh so beautiful. Harold nodded again. Oh yes, she would suit him very well.

The slave master pulled the clamps to demonstrate how the nipples could be moved up down or around and still cause no damage to the goods. He and the auctioneer had worked together for many years and had done well in their merchandising of human flesh. Now they were dressed in the fine rich raiments of merchants. The goods they enjoyed the most were the girls destined to be the sex slaves.

Harold cast his dark intelligent eyes back to the Prince in his ornate carriage across the square. He was smiling. Handsome, with fine delicate features, the Prince was supposedly desperate for an heir. If the girl was truly of noble birth that would suit the Prince very well. A shame the man was destined to be disappointed.

"Megan, my dear," whispered Harold, "would you care to have that fair beauty as your newest toy?" He could let Megan play her little games and see how she behaved. If Zacora seemed to be suitable in every way, he mused, then he would see.

Fascinated, her mouth open with delight, Megan was staring at the podium. The slave master was demonstrating how the girl was fully broken in for sexual pleasure.

"The story, ladies and gentlemen, will amuse you." The slave master was kneeling at Zacora's feet, his neatly trimmed beard close to but not touching her open sex. "She claims that she was tricked by a young squire who took her virginity."

The crowd sniggered as they watched the slave master use both hands to open the plump silver fronded sex lips. He urged the girl to widen her long legs and bend them to give him full access. It was very moist and he slicked a finger through the parted lips, holding it up for the crowd to see. He then held up a smooth wooden peg, polished and dark, almost but not quite imitating a man's penis. "Observe, ladies and gentlemen," he said, "that she has been fully prepared for service."

The crowd was silent, waiting and craning forward, eager to see the fair slave demonstrated. The girl's eyes were wide and moist with unshed tears, Harold noticed, but she stood quite still and proud. She might be humiliated by the slave master's actions, but she seemed to accept them willingly, as though she had been trained to do so. He liked that. He liked that very much.

The slave master, in his richly hued satin, knelt with thighs spread at the slave's feet. Even at this distance across the square Harold could see the man's erect cock spearing upwards under the robe. Even the slave master, with his vast experience of girls destined to be sexual playthings, was excited by Zacora's compliance.

The polished rod of wood was offered upwards by the slave master, like a relic to some sensual god. He held it reverently in both hands against the peachy smoothness of the girl's shivering belly. She looked straight ahead while the slave master was intent upon his task. Many girls would have sobbed or screamed at this humiliation, but Zacora seemed to expect it. It was part of her life, Harold could tell.

Now the polished phallus slid back down her belly, very slowly, stroking the fine silk until the wood reached the downy softness of the silvery bush.

There was not a whisper in the crowd. Harold had never seen them so intent upon the slave podium. The other girls, darker, shorter, not quite so beautiful but attractive enough, were shuffling restlessly in their light chains.

The gleaming rod, so smoothly polished by a skilled craftsman, entered the girl, pressing back the sex folds firmly with its girth. Harold could see a trickle of the girl's lubrication ooze down the hard stem. Her face was passive, showing no expression apart from the gleam in the sapphire blue eyes and a slight parting of moist lips. This was nothing new to her, Harold realised. He saw the mound jut forward a little, the fronds parting to show the swelling inner lips and the pert bud hugely erect for all to see.

In the square there was silence apart from quickened breathing amongst the crowd and the occasional metallic chink of the slave's chains. Harold, himself, leaned from his carriage, with Megan at his side.

"Can we have her?" said Megan. Her plump breasts, rising from her brief dress, were flushed with excitement and they rose and fell rapidly.

"I've said so, haven't I?" His tone was terse, for his male sword was painful in its wanting. "But we must see how the auction goes."

"Oh, we'll outbid anyone here," said Megan confidently.

Harold nodded to the soft featured Prince, gazing longingly at the girl. "Don't be too sure," he said.

Megan tossed her head in disdain and turned to more interesting sights on the podium. The blonde girl, hair streaming in soft shimmering coils down her naked back, was in the full throes of orgasm. The polished wooden rod was slicking back and forth, in and out of the girl's convulsing entrance.

Harold groaned softly in delight as he saw the phallus withdrawn and held up to the crowd. It was thickly coated with the girl's love sap. She gave a soft whimper of pleasure. Her chained wrists were linked behind her head and Harold saw them tighten as she reached her peak.

The crowd gave a communal sigh and the slave master rose to his feet, holding the steaming phallus in his raised hands. Everyone could see the liquid from the depths of the girl's body dripping hotly down the slave master's raised arms.

A great cheer went up and, seeing the enthusiasm which the slave master's demonstration raised, the auctioneer stepped forward, anxious to start the bidding while so much interest was aroused.

"Zacora," he introduced, pulling the blonde girl forward by a thin gold chain decorating her waist. "Of noble birth, so we are told and betrayed by a noble young squire." The last few words brought scattered laughter among the crowd.

Harold's eyes did not leave the girl's willowy, but ripe, figure. Zacora, he breathed. Even her name was beautiful, mystical, magic. The deep sapphire eyes stared over the heads of the crowd, the soft lips parted and moist. The proud breasts were high, forced so by the position of her arms behind her head. The nipples were pinched by the silver devices held by cunning clips and teeth.

The auctioneer traced the gentle curve of the waist, so cleverly enhanced by the simple addition of the gold chain. He stroked the tiny swell of the belly before turning her round to sweep his hands over the fullness of the bottom cheeks, parting them to show the tight pinkness of the rear mouth with delicate wrinkles like the spokes of a wheel. "Tight, you see, ladies and gentlemen," he said, "so wonderfully tight."

The bottom mouth flexed involuntarily and Harold felt his groin tense. He loved the secretiveness of buttocks in a beautiful girl. There was something forbidden about their loveliness which he found it hard to resist.

The girl was made to open her mouth, to draw out her tongue to show its pink cleanliness. The auctioneer nodded to the slave master as a signal.

The slave master lifted his richly woven robe to expose the magnificence of his penis. Zacora was pushed to her knees and her mouth was forced wide. The satiny globe, slick and purple, was pressed into the available orifice. It seemed to Harold that the shaft was being swallowed eagerly as the girl massaged the tightness of the rim with her soft lips. The agile tongue flicked back and forth over the slipperiness until, very slowly, the thick girth was swallowed and Zacora's soft lips nestled in the crisp curls of the slave master's pubis.

A communal sigh of satisfaction was drawn from the crowd. Zacora's lips slid up and down the thick shaft, caressing it at each slick passage. She gave his sperm sac a pat with her tongue at the end of a caress. The magnificent organ began to throb and, suddenly, he pulled from her, turning to the crowd and holding his shaft proudly in both hands. A great fountain shot from it, splashing the nearest onlookers with hot, creamy jets.

Zacora, head held proudly and hands linked in her tumbled hair, allowed the slave master's spillage to lie upon her pale cheeks. A pearly droplet hung upon her soft lower lip and she sucked it lovingly into her mouth.

"A thousand drachma!" The voice was loud, urgent.

The crowd looked towards its source. A Prince in a suit of cloth of gold and a solid gold codpiece stood close to the podium. He held a leather bag, thrusting it at the auctioneer.

"Two thousand!" Harold remained in his carriage, unlike the anxious Prince.

Bidding became fast and furious. No such sums had been taken for sex slaves before. The crowd murmured delightedly. It reached thirty-five thousand and the Prince shook his head as he walked dejectedly to his carriage. The horses were whipped furiously by the driver and the carriage scattered the crowd as it hurtled from the scene.

"We got her!" exclaimed Megan. Her plump figure, covered only by a very brief black silk dress, jiggled excitedly. Her breasts were fighting each other under the silk like warring little animals. "I'll use her to teach my clients a few new games."

Megan, much to Harold's disapproval, had set herself up as part-time harlot. "It's a hobby," she told him. "I'm not efficient as a housekeeper, so I can't help you very much round the castle and I've got have something to keep me out of mischief." It went much against the grain to agree for it did not help Harold's social standing in Vakir and he had ambition, great ambition. The Meleagans would be the top family in the land before very much longer. He had sworn an oath to that.

"Yes, my dear," replied Harold at last. "It has been a very satisfying morning." He turned to Megan's son. "Gareth, my boy, order a sedan to pick up the slave first thing in the morning."

"Why is it always me?" grumbled Gareth.

CHAPTER THREE

Zacora watched the carriage drive away from the market place. The audience, too, slowly drifted to the neighbouring villages, leaving debris of rotting fruit, mouldering in the hot sun. She sighed. It was all so different to the tranquil existence she had led before.

"What are you waiting for, stuck up bitch?" hissed a voice behind her.

She looked round. One of the other girls, small, dark and scowling with venom, was glaring up at her. "Suppose you think you're something because you fetched a big price."

Zacora shrugged miserably, her eyes lowered.

"Well, you're not, see." The girl, quick and lithe, slipped her hands, manacled with the links of chain, around Zacora's slender body, catching the nipples in the links. The pain made tears glaze the sapphire eyes, but Zacora kicked backwards, feeling her toes sink into moist sex flesh.

"Stop that, you hellcats!" boomed the slave master. A whip snaked around the two struggling young naked bodies. "Get down to the cells to await transport." The whip lashed again as the two girls disentangled themselves, catching Zacora across the softness of her breasts and the other girl across her small pert buttocks. The lash struck again, not for any other reason than to give the slave master pleasure.

The cells were dark and cavernous. A jailer greeted the group of girls as the slave master ushered them into the rank filth of the cells.

"Auction finished?" The jailer, wearing only a scrap of worn leather, gathered to a pouch, looked up smiling. He scratched at his groin with a huge key hanging from a bunch on his wrist.

"Get this place cleaned up," ordered the slave master. "It stinks."

The jailer, a huge man, shrugged, using the key to scratch his long, thick greasy hair. "Don't matter. Slaves don't matter."

"They matter a great deal!" yelled the slave master, so loudly that the noise, echoing through the stone cells, made Zacora's ears ring. "They are sold goods. They have to stay in good condition."

Zacora felt a rough hand close upon her upper arm. She flinched, looking up into the grinning dark face of the jailer.

"This is an unusual one," the big man hissed. "All these golden curls and this..." He caressed the fluff of her pubic bush.

Zacora stiffened, but the soft silver curls of her mound were automatically thrust forward. Her long legs, muscles tense and nervous, were splayed as far apart as her ankle manacles allowed.

The jailer cupped Zacora's sex, stroking the valleys where her thighs met the silver fronded lips. "Nice and full," he remarked, "for such a slender girl." He slid the flat of his palm along the lips, so delicately sprinkled with fine silver curls. "A virgin, I suppose?" He consulted a list given to him by the slave master. "Must be at this price. Thirty-five thousand! A record, isn't it?"

The slave master nodded. "It's a record to be sure, but she isn't a virgin."

"She isn't?" A heavy sheen of perspiration broke out on the jailer's face and body and his rough fingers prised open the fullness of Zacora's sex lips, feeling the slippery coating of sex sap oozing along her folds.

"Lost her virginity to a noble's son, stupid wench!" sneered the slave master. "So she ended up here. Told some lies about being betrothed to him." But Zacora looked back at the slave master proudly, knowing the truth of her terrible betrayal.

"The Meleagan sedan will pick her up first thing in the morning," the slave master advised the jailer, who was licking his lips with eagerness.

The other bought slaves slumped down against old walls, slimy with oozing damp and green with a heavy growth of algae. Some settled down to sleep as they waited to be taken to their new owner's homes and some sobbed quietly, making the chains which held them captive rattle metallically. Only Zacora stood proudly, as still as a statue.

The jailer circled round her, his rough, gnarled hands reaching out to touch when he noticed a part of her body which interested him. The smooth under swell of her breasts attracted him first and she tried very hard not to flinch when a clawlike finger stroked upwards to the nipple. She even tried to smile, for he was, after all, a man, and as such, should be welcomed by her.

"You like to be caressed, my beauty," he croaked. "Do you not?"

"It is my duty to accept it, sir." Her smile was tremulous and uncertain. The jailer was not like any man she had met before. He was filthy. His hair was unkempt and thick with grease. The teeth remaining in his mouth were broken or black with rot, but his physique told her that he was young and very virile. His life, down here in the darkness of the damp cells, had aged him beyond his years.

"I knew you liked it when I touched your cunt," he croaked. "It was wet; dripping wet."

"I am trained to give pleasure to a man," she said softly.

"So you'll pleasure me?" The jailer's voice was barely audible. He grasped her breasts, massaging them cruelly and pinching their nipples. The gnarled hands went down to her belly, squeezing the taut flesh and digging one finger into the depths of her naval.

Her smile was unwavering. Her sapphire blue eyes remained soft and inviting. The lithe body bent to his will, allowing him to touch it as it pleased him.

"Answer me, wench?" he said loudly, lifting her hand and clipping her ear.

All her training taught her that she should answer him and agree with his request to be pleasured, but his odour was unclean and, although his body was young, his demeanour was old, as old as Satan himself.

Zacora remained still, her smile there but fading. They were suspended in time as she pondered on how to answer him.

"Very well then," he said, before she could speak. "I must teach you a lesson in how to behave with your betters, since you seem to have forgotten your training."

The golden hair was grabbed into a thick hank and a small mew of pain escaped her lips as she was dragged across the filthy straw-strewn floor. Through tear-blurred eyes she saw other girls taking notice, waking from sleep or wiping faces streaked from weeping. The small dark girl who had showed so much envy when they were brought to the cells was pointing a finger which mocked.

"Miss High and Mighty is truly fallen," she sneered. She thrust her pelvis forward, lewdly opening her sex lips to show the contents and thrust a finger quickly in and out. "That's what you'll get from that old bastard," she laughed, "except it won't be quite so comfortable as my finger."

"Shut up, bitch!" the jailer growled.

They reached a low platform and he threw Zacora on to it. The manacles and chains at ankles and wrists made it easy to fasten her to a strange device which brooded there, sinister and waiting for a victim. Within seconds he had hooked her to bolts upon it and her arms and legs were widely splayed. Even on the gallows, in clear sight of everyone in the castle, she had not felt so vulnerable and open as she did in the clutch of this wicked machine.

The dark girl came to look down on her, touching her intimately and laughing. "You've got her now," she gloated. Roughly, the girl slid two fingers into the well-splayed folds of Zacora's sex. She pulled them out again, looking at them in the smokey light of a tallow candle. "If she's scared she doesn't show it," she said, stroking the running juices with her other hand.

The vulnerability which Zacora felt was enhanced by the strange device. On it she seemed more open and defenceless than ever before.

"Turn the handle," begged the girl. "Let me hear her scream. Stuck up, bitch!"

It was only then that Zacora realised that she was on a rack, one of the most diabolical instruments of torture ever devised. How far would the jailer dare to go with it? If she died her new owner wouldn't be pleased. He'd paid a fortune.

"Witch!" rasped the jailer, rebuking the dark girl. "Are you mad? I'm not turning that handle."

The girl looked disappointed. "Then why've you put her there?" she wanted to know. "Waste of time."

"You will see!" The jailer deftly untied the thong which held his pouch in place, releasing an organ magnificent in size, but horribly grimed with dust and caked semen. It was erect and the eye gleamed with a pearl of his seed.

"No!" said Zacora.

The jailer had leapt between her long splayed thighs and was slicking his hands up and down the spearing thickness.

"You dare to defy me, my beauty?"

There was little humiliation which Zacora would not take. Her behavioural training encompassed everything, but she would not, could not, take this monstrous unclean penis into her body.

"Whip her into submission first," advised the girl.

"No," the jailer grinned. "Turn the handle after all. Only three notches, mind."

"Oh, yes!" hissed the girl gleefully. She took the handle in both her small hands, her face a mask of spiteful joy.

"No more than three," murmured the jailer again. A drool of spittle made a slow trail through the grime of his unshaven but roughly handsome face. His tongue flicked around his lips as he looked down at the golden beauty, stretched out at his mercy. She hid her fear well, for the deep blue eyes stared up at him proudly, daring him to do his worst.

The golden body was so mouth-watering, splayed out openly below him, that he knew not where to start. Deep in thought, he stroked the heaviness of his balls, feeling their weight and readiness. Never had there been such a beauty at his disposal. They were all the dark tough little women of Vakir, bought for the vulgar work in their master's houses. Bossy in the extreme, sex with them made him feel inferior.

Very occasionally a virgin would be brought to auction; fair of skin and subservient like this one lying there tightly stretched upon the rack beneath him. But they were out of bounds for him. They were virgins, too valuable to be used by a mere jailer.

Except for this one!

His penis throbbed as he looked at the open flesh of the woman's sex. The lips were swollen, inflamed and parted. The silver curls were sparse and neatly trimmed, making the contents of the pouch more available. The inner lips fluttered, which, he had heard, was a feature of the women from Lokara. They were trained to pleasure a man to the full by petting his cock with these highly mobile lips. He shuddered with desire, reaching into the wet depths just as the little dark maid pulled on the handle to engage the third notch.

The sound of the ratchet was loud, echoing through the vast cell block. Only a tiny mew of pain came from the splayed girl. They usually screamed loud and long, even the men. He felt a flood of sap soak his intruding finger. A smile creased his uncouth features. She was enjoying herself.

The long creamy arms were splayed wide, stretched to the limit. The legs, too, were taut. This had the effect of hollowing the belly and he caressed the deep cleft of the naval, pressing it inwards and feeling the softness of the organs beneath. The mound, delicately fleshed and decorated with silver curls, pouted upwards. This again was the effect of the rack, stretching the fine bones of the beautiful pelvis.

Against his orders the ratchet engaged a fourth time, and he thought he saw a flicker of panic in the girl's eyes, but it was only momentary. The pride returned to the beautiful face and the soft lips parted in a most inviting manner.

Two fingers were easily accommodated at the soft liquid entrance and the inner lips gave a cossetting caress to the uninvited digits.

Yet another notch clicked on the rack. It was done in a spitefully quick manner and Zacora made a soft moan. "Prissy bitch!" the dark girl spat. "Sex is sex. We don't make a religion out of it here."

"More's the pity!" said the jailer, pushing three fingers fully to the hilt into Zacora's fluttering sex purse, revelling in its wetness and pampering cushion of its walls.

For a while his rough hands roved over her tight frame, glorying in its tenseness, its inability to avoid his intimate probing, the way his crude mauling of her body seemed to excite her further, whether she wanted it or no.

"She's ready now!" he exulted at last.

He thrust three fingers into her. "Yes!" he breathed, adding a fourth finger to the other three. "Ready!" His thumb balled the tip of Zacora's clitoris, feeling its throbbing heat.

Zacora's mind hated the thought of the man's filthy penis entering her. So recently the lordly Ogham took her virginity and now she must submit to a shaft which water had never touched. She looked at its thickness, its throbbing length and she felt herself pulse around his roughly invading fingers. The pulsing was involuntary. Her mind may have hated the thought of the penis penetrating her, but her body was ready to welcome it.

He took her hair and twisted her face to his.

"You want it, don't you?"

"Oh God!" she panted, "Oh yes. Fuck me!"

He laughed at the crude words coming from the angelic mouth; from a girl who looked like an angel. "Say it again. Tell me what you want." He was kneeling between the thighs which were painfully stretched by the rack, towering over her, his penis spearing high and held in his hands.

"Fuck me!" she gasped. Her breasts, flattened by the tension of the rack, were still enticing mounds with mouth watering nipples as red as cherries. He fell upon her, taking them, in turn, into his mouth. They were grated sharply by the broken teeth.

The smooth heat of his tip lay nestling in the midst of her folds, teasing her needful flesh as his hands and mouth painfully took their fill of her body. The thick length inched into her vagina. It seemed that it was the only part of her which was mobile and free. It was not shackled or stretched to the very limits of bearable pain. She felt her own moisture soaking the invading shaft and seeping down her spread buttock cheeks on to the rough wood of the ancient rack. Natural, and taught, instinct was to gyrate around the male shaft, but she was held still, immobile and helpless. The only answer was to caress the hardness of his cock with her own muscular, cushiony walls.

"Aaargh!" grunted the jailer. His body was imbued with a pleasure which was almost unbearable in its intensity. He levered himself on her stretched arms, increasing the pain in the joints and, again, thrust into her. A whisper of pleasure escaped her soft mouth. It was a breath as soft as a child's in its mother's arms. Her freshly opened passage caressed the invading hardness, welcoming it as part of her own body. The two, the unlikely couple, were moulded as one.

The pleasure which she gave him was too much for a prolonged taking on his part. He began to pulse wildly and she knew that he would spurt his seed into her helpless body. Her clitoris was jerking wildly with each pump of his thickness into her. A swirling heat in her belly and that wonderful spiral of passion in the whole of her helpless body took her high above the pain of the rack. She was consumed with a climax within which nothing else mattered.

The jailer groaned, giving a final grind of his coarse crotch as he thrust deep into her. The first wave of his climax was so pleasurable it seemed heaven-sent. He felt his cock swell, as though it would burst, and a great gush of hot seed spumed into her, spilling out to back-flow along his own length. And again the pleasure wave came. If anything, it was greater than the last. His irrigation of her flooded more copiously. And again he was hit with the consuming fire of his orgasm, until he thought he would die from the pleasure waves.

Satiated at last he collapsed upon Zacora's tightly fettered body, straining every joint in the girl's tortured limbs. Tiny mews of pain escaped her parted lips, but she could not escape the jailer's muscular weight.

His penis remained inside her, resting hotly in her still convulsing vagina. Awash with juices, hers and his, she could feel the thick, warm cocktail oozing over the sensitised cheeks of her spread buttocks.

His horny hands grasped her breasts, digging rough uncut finger nails into the tender flesh. More than anything she wanted to be free from the weight of him; free from his fetid breath and yet, had she not enjoyed his taking? Had she not enjoyed the flood of his spume into her? Did he not take away the thoughts of the terrible pain of the rack, or rather combine it with the pleasure of his fucking?

At last he lifted himself. His movements were slow and lethargic, as though he had run a great distance. "Are you some kind of witch to drain so much energy from a man?" he growled. He splashed the copious dew lingering on his penis across her prone body. She felt its heat on her face and breasts and felt it trickle over her stretched skin.

"No, sir," she whispered politely. "It is my training which makes your pleasure so great."

He grinned, scratching his heavy sperm sac as he walked to the side of the rack. She felt a release of the painful tension as he let go the ratchets. "Later in the night," he chuckled. "you can use that training once more, but I must rest." He looked down at her, admiring the pale, willowy beauty with the crown of golden hair. "This is a rare treat, my lovely, a rare treat."

"Thank you, sir," She gave him one of her inviting, shy smiles.

"How anyone could be so beautiful, so innocent and yet so sexually skilled," he said, shaking his greasy head, "beats me."

He walked away, still shaking his head in wonder, and heaped the straw where he slept.

Zacora, her limbs cramped and sore, swallowed hard. "Sir?" she said diffidently.

"What is it?" He spoke in a gruff growl.

"Could you, perhaps, release me, so that I might sleep?"

"Be quiet," he rasped. "Sleep where you are. I'm not taking the chance of an expensive item like you trying to escape. More than my life's worth. The punishment mistress would flay me alive."

The cells were dark, silent and dank as the night deepened. Cold seeped like sharp knives into Zacora's tortured joints. The copious silky wetness of the jailer's seed mixed with her own sex sap cooled on her outspread thighs. Sleep was impossible on the discomfort of the rack and hot tears tumbled across her pale cheeks.

CHAPTER FOUR

At first the guards seemed a little afraid of her. They eyed her suspiciously. Kept casting nervous glances at her slender nakedness, at her shining sapphire eyes, the pale hair, the peachy skin. The women of their country were dark swarthy and well-built, almost masculine in appearance and behaviour, whereas Zacora was so feminine, pliant and passive.

One of the guards, called Wolf by his friends, told her that she seemed to them fairy-like, so fragile in spite of her long athletic limbs, that if they touched her she would break or dissolve like a will o' the wisp.

"Are you sure you're not magic?" he asked her on the first night of their long journey. Zacora saw him looking longingly at the tautness of her pale breasts with the delicately flushed nipple centred so perfectly in each mound.

Zacora was silent, looking at his huge frame lit by the flickering camp fire. The guards had been ordered that they were on no account to unshackle her, and one of them must always accompany her when she went to the bushes to perform natural functions.

"No," she told him, fixing her soft gaze on his raised and parted knees. "I'm not a fairy or a witch or anything magical. In my country all the girls are fair of skin and hair."

Wolf licked his lips. "You must obey me. Do everything I say," he said almost nervously.

"I know." Zacora lowered her eyes as was the custom in the far off land from which she came.

The big man gulped. He wasn't used to women who were passive; who did what they were told. Here, in Vakir, the women were the masters. He gritted his teeth angrily. It was all the fault of that wretched Prince; that weakling.

"I'm going to feel your sex," he said, trying to keep his deep voice steady. "Lie back and keep your legs open."

Zacora saw the other three guards shuffle across from their seating places round the camp fire to look more closely. Wolf's words set up the familiar glow in her belly, the warm softness which she always felt in intimacy. A gentle smile, beckoning and welcoming, hovered around her lips.

"Will you scream?" asked Wolf.

Zacora shook her head. She knew her sex was wet and ready, as it always was at the promise of the touch of a stranger, specially when she was naked and chained.

"Hands above your head," said Wolf. His voice was barely audible, whispering and husky. He watched Zacora's shackled hands, pale and long-fingered, go obediently to a point above her shining head.

The shackles were attached to a long chain which caressed the length of her creamy body. Wolf swayed the loose links over the pouting mounds of her breasts, watching colour suffuse the pale skin. He sat back on his haunches and Zacora could see his male flesh lengthening beneath the square of leather of his loin cloth. She looked away, only to be given sight of three more dark sex swords, swaying and stiffening.

Wolf's dusky middle finger probed between the silver puff of curls on her female mound. "Open your legs wide," he grunted, "as far as chain will allow."

Her ankle manacles were chained, but the chain allowed her to straddle her legs to full stretch. The body chain rubbed across her warm flesh at every breath. It was taut, stretching from her wrist manacles to the chain between her ankles.

Wolf, also breathing hard, moved to her head, carrying a heavy rock. She looked up at him, the deep blue eyes desperate with fear, but he smiled at her, holding up a stout twig. "To peg you to the ground, my beauty."

"But I said I wouldn't scream," she reminded him. In her mind she could feel the brush of his rough finger against the silky curls on her sex.

"Brad, Pike and Kroll are big men," he said with a smile which was part cruel and part apologetic.

"But you are the biggest," sneered Pike, lifting Wolf's loin cloth.

Zacora gasped. A shaft, almost ebony black, gleaming with its skin stretched tight over the bloated contents rose up from a crisply curled groin. She listened to the steady knocking as the big man banged the stick into the spongy woodland ground. The wrist chain was secured to the earth, making her more helpless than ever.

Her breasts pouted upwards, cleaved by the chain between them. With every pound of the rock they seemed to become fuller and tighter. There was more moisture slicking the pink inner folds of her sex.

Another tough twig was pounded in the earth between her straddled legs. She was helpless, just as she had been with the noble. A heat came from nowhere and entered her naked belly, making her melt inside while her clitoris became engorged.

The men, the four men, slid their loin cloths to the side, baring the stiffness of their male weapons. They were lit by the flickering flames of the camp fire, and, silhouetted against their dark bodies, they looked bigger and more menacing than ever.

Chained and staked though she was, Zacora felt a fever of excitement, a forbidden delight at being naked and so open and vulnerable at the men's feet. She gave them a slight smile, curving her soft lips and parting them sweetly.

Wolf frowned. "The woman is a harlot," he said harshly. "She beckons us." He bent down to look at the open moistness of the silver fronded sex lips. "You see!" he said triumphantly. "How her flesh seeps sap, ready for taking!"

"You don't understand!" cried Zacora. "In my country women must smile at men or they are whipped." Unshed tears glazed the lustrous eyes. "Only twice has my body been taken. I could not prevent it, for I was tethered - as now."

Wolf grinned. "In your country, they know how to treat women!" The other men laughed. "Here, we men must suffer all manner of humiliation by women. Only on such a task as this are we able to take advantage and give as good as we get."

The man called Pike had cut several long twigs from a willow and was binding them together.

"Where first?"

Wolf caressed the prone body with his eyes, gazing long and hard between the splayed legs where the skin gleamed silkily and a jutting scarlet bud probed from silver fronds. The breasts were tempting, swollen. The slight swell of the belly sweeping down to the triangle of silver blonde curls tempted him, but then perhaps it would be better to have her pegged face down, to thrash her buttocks. He nodded to himself, making the decision.

"See if we can roll her on to her belly," he said. "I think the body chain has enough slack."

Rough hands dug cruelly into the flesh of her upper arms and thighs as they rolled her over. The body chain cut into the flesh of the valley between her full breasts, her belly and mound. The new position made the tension on her shoulder sockets much greater and the pale flesh of her breasts was pressed into the soft leafy ground.

"Better," murmured Wolf. "Much better." His big hands cupped the fullness of her bottom, stroking the lower curves and leading up to the parted crease.

"Give me the willow twigs." Wolf's voice was low, trembling with excitement.

Zacora glanced over her creamy shoulder. Wolf was looking at the place between her splayed thighs with the flushed pink flesh, shining with moisture and centred by a delicate bud which she knew thrust out at him. He stroked the very ends of the willow twigs across the parted hemispheres, making Zacora shiver as she wondered at her fate. Part of her was supremely excited. She felt light headed at her vulnerable predicament; pegged to the ground and held by chains. She knew that Wolf and the other men could see every detail of her sex pouch, every fold, every moist crease, but she could not see anything of theirs.

The still evening air was disturbed by the swish of the crude whip, but only the very tips brushed the lower curves of her parted buttocks. It was a tickle, a brush, a taste of what she knew was to come. Her hands grasped at the peg which held her wrists to the ground and her slim body tensed as she waited for blows yet to be received.

Silently, her soft lips parted, she mouthed a prayer of thanks to her teachers. It was they who had shown her how to be disciplined and take punishment; it was they who taught her to be passive and obedient to all men.

Her buttock flesh quivered as the willow whip struck in earnest. A faint mew of surprise whispered from her lips.

"See how the flesh reddens," said the man called Kroll. "Each twig gives a thin stripe of scarlet."

"Again," whispered Pike. "Do it again."

The lash beat down again, harder this time, and Zacora's body arched involuntarily, bowing upwards from the mossy ground.

Was she being punished for all the humiliation that the men suffered in their own land? She could think of no other reason for them to treat her so harshly.

A rough finger slipped into the hot moistness of her naked and vulnerable sex, displayed so openly by her position on the leafy ground.

The finger slipped into her easily, sliding between the folds without resistance. Zacora felt her face flush, remembering what Wolf had called her earlier. A harlot. The word echoed in her mind, but she wasn't, surely she wasn't.

"Her sex sap flows readily," said Wolf, "and her passage is open."

Zacora felt a work roughened thumb graze over the pouting erection of her clitoris. She heard herself sigh, whispering her pleasure at the touch on that sensitive place. She bore down on the intruding fingers, for that was what she was taught to do for men. She must receive both pleasure and pain gladly, for that was what men required to obtain full release.

"The bitch asks to be taken," said Wolf roughly. "What does she need?"

"Punishment!" said the others with one voice.

Zacora tensed, knowing what was coming. Her buttocks were greatly heated from the first lash of the willow whip. She felt that the tender flesh had been peppered with coarse sand, for there were many points of pain.

The pain was greatly enhanced at the next blow. The heat suffused her whole body as well as making her buttocks a swelling mound of fire. Tears welled up in her sapphire eyes, spilling down the peach-like cheeks to add to the dampness of the fallen forest leaves. Her soft lips curved to a perfect O as breath was forced from them.

"She likes the pain," said Brad, excitement obvious in his voice.

It was true. In Lokara women were taught to accept discipline. But there, it was controlled pain; an exciting prelude to a man's taking of their flesh.

"Please, not so hard," she whispered. She looked over her shoulder, her limpid eyes seeking Wolf's dark brown ones, pleading for less harsh discipline. "Make the strokes lighter and I shall gladly take you into my body."

Squatting by her helpless body, Wolf stroked his fingers across the inflamed hillocks of her bottom. She could see the beauty of his male shaft, erect and spearing from between his massive brown thighs. His gaze was fixed on her parted buttocks. He allowed his fingers to trace each line left by the willow twigs, feeling the welt where the flesh was raised.

"Lightly, you say?" he queried. He frowned into the blueness of her eyes.

"Yes," she murmured. "If the pain brings tears, how can I take your bodies gladly?"

Tense, her hands clasped tightly around the peg which held her wrist chains and her legs spread taut and wide, Zacora waited. Her bottom was a mound of fire, but her sex was delicately flushed, almost ready for the penetration which she knew would follow the beating. Her sex sap gathered on the pink and swollen folds, moistening her bud which was jerking involuntarily, pouting for attention.

The willow twigs whispered through the air. Zacora licked her lips in that interminably long second as she waited for the blow to fall. It came. Upon the pain already inflicted, it stung hotly, adding to the raised welts lifting on the pert mounds.

Men are my masters, thought Zacora. It has always been so in Lokara. As the willow twigs swished through the warm night air and she waited for the next blow, she thought back to her home, the castle where she was born; the noble knight who took her virginity and, when he had finished with her, sent her to the auction to be sold.

"She makes not a sound," said Brad, marvelling at Zacora's silence.

"Except the sighs of passion," added Pike. "Is it now, Wolf? Can we take the woman's body now?"

A hard naked toe prodded the softness of her breast, the full flesh sloping into the leafy forest floor. "Aye," rasped Kroll, "and who shall be first?"

Zacora looked up at him. His square jaw jutted forward belligerently as he looked down at her. He stroked the smoothness of his erection, iron in its rigidity. He grinned and posed his shaft at her, thrusting his muscular pelvis forward and cupping the hard fullness of his balls.

Zacora turned away, although all her training had taught her that she should have smiled at a man who desired her. She had no wish to be called a harlot again.

The hard toe prodded the fullness of her breasts again. "Would you wish me to be first, my pretty?" asked Kroll.

She could see the bloated veins of his rigidity pulsing with eagerness. A pearly dew drop hung upon the bloated globe of his penis, shimmering in the light of the dying fire. "If you wish," she said, but her voice was cold and polite. There was no warmth of invitation.

He kicked her again. "The wench is insolent," he said spitefully.

Wolf laughed. "And our women are not?" he questioned. "Apart from Harold the Pretender and the Prince there is not a man in Vakir who can stand up to our women. Enjoy the good manners of this one while you may."

Kroll grunted sullenly. "No more whipping?" he said, feeling that his spite should be vented in some way.

Fingers, cool compared from the fire in her buttocks, touched the thousand raised welts on the once creamy skin. Zacora trembled at the touch, wanting them to enter the darkness of the cleft between her buttocks and go further. She wanted them to cosset the spongy moistness which awaited in her willing sex pouch.

"Turn her over," said Wolf, and she heard him throw the willow whip to the floor.

As she was turned upon her back she winced as tiny twigs and pebbles on the forest floor pressed into the punished flesh of her buttocks. With the four huge men looking down on her, she was suddenly ashamed of her nakedness. This emotion had never plagued her before, for she was proud of her body, but she knew they looked upon her in a different light from the men of Lokara.

Her breasts were swollen on each side of the body chain, pouting out with nipples inflamed and massively erect. Zacora closed her eyes, not wishing to look upon her own body. It had suddenly become a thing of shame rather than a supple living thing of beauty.

A roughened nail flicked each pert nipple, making shots of pain flutter through the taut mounds. She winced, opening the sapphire blue eyes wide, questioning the reason for such outright cruelty.

"Isn't it a great feeling?" Wolf hissed. "Tonight we are the masters!"

Pike gave a gleeful growl. "The masters," he echoed. "Our issue will not be banked to produce yet more women. The masters, if only for tonight!"

Zacora held her breath in shock. Every muscle in her slender body became tense with horror. What kind of hell was this?

"If the Prince could produce a son, an heir," sighed Wolf, "perhaps there would be kindness in the land once more. Perhaps there would be love between men and women. Perhaps life would be normal."

Brad and Pike nodded. "We were spared only because we were strong and were suitable for hard manual labour." Brad looked down at her, cruelty and revenge patent in his dark eyes.

Zacora was beginning to understand. The men, those which were spared, hated women. They punished them for being women whenever there was a chance. A pliant and passive beauty, obedient and eager to please was a treat which they could not resist.

Stretched tautly above her head, Zacora's arms ached intolerably. Her bottom was raw and inflamed. She remained still, so that it would not chafe on the forest floor. Her sex, so naked and unprotected, felt very vulnerable. At home, with her own kind, she would have revelled in that very vulnerability.

"It is time," said Wolf, kneeling between her splayed legs and feeling the plumpness of her mound, stroking the perfectly rounded arch of her pubis. She felt the soft pad of flesh ripple under his fingers and the silver curls of her bush whisper against his palm.

The circling moons, the three sisters as the locals called them, had risen and shed cold light upon the scene. The mens' bodies gleamed darkly in the pale light. Their huge chests, with the massively developed pectorals, were a mass of shadows and highlights. The tight stomachs and narrow hips were firm. Long shadowed thighs and huge calves were straddled wide and their male sex swords were thrust forward eagerly. Zacora found her eyes straying to the heavy sacs, so full and taut under the arches of the splayed thighs. If the men were so deprived of affection, of sex, those sacs must be bursting to release their contents. She found herself shuddering uncontrollably.

Thumbs spread the plump moist folds wide open, making her even more exposed and vulnerable. "Never have I seen a woman's sex so pale," whispered Wolf. "Always they are dark. And this one has such a dainty bud, so young and innocent."

The compliments were obviously sincere and Zacora found herself smiling with pleasure, in spite of the possible insults she might rain down upon herself.

"Now she preens!" scoffed Brad. "Penetrate her to the hilt."

The sharp words were said spitefully. Tears blurred Zacora's vision and, again, she felt ashamed of her body. Even when she lost her virginity, she did not feel shame or humiliation, but somehow these men made her feel dirty with their actions and words.

Kroll stroked the fan of golden hair spread around her beautiful face, tracing the silver highlights caught by the light of the three moons. He was squatting behind her head and she looked back at him, trying again to please, but the smile was rewarded by a hard slap across the cheeks. Zacora gasped for the blow was a shock and a surprise. It made her head rock against her arms, stretched so tightly behind her. And again the blow was repeated, this time with the back of Kroll's hard hand. Zacora's beautiful face burned with shame and the force of the blow.

Wolf looked up. His fingers investigated every moist crevice of her sex and she could feel a melting in the lower part of her belly and she knew it heralded the beginnings of her orgasm. "She's getting wet," he said, grinning at the other men. He pointed a free hand at Kroll. "Hey! Don't damage her, idiot."

Face burning, Zacora looked up at Kroll, asking why with wide blue eyes. He dived his rough hand into the depths of her silky hair, tugging her head back until her long creamy throat was exposed. The action lifted her breasts, arching them high and making her nipples more available to him.

"It hurts," she whispered softly, trying vainly to release his grip by twisting her head from side to side, but this only increased the pain.

"You talk too much," he rasped, tugging her hair yet harder. "We must find some way to close your mouth." He looked at Wolf, seeking permission.

Wolf grinned, nodding before returning to his task of stimulating the girl.

A further tug in her long golden hair brought Kroll's face close to hers. She could feel her sex aching for pleasure. She knew the folds were swollen and open for Wolf's attention. She knew her bud was fully exposed and it was jutting upwards from the moistness of the flushed bed. She felt ugly and used in her humiliation, but at the same time she didn't want Wolf to stop his caresses.

She heard him snigger and she heard a metallic rattle. The body chain was loose, dangling somewhere over her head. She couldn't see it because Kroll still held her by the hair. Although the opportunity was there because the lower end of the body chain was released, she had no wish to close her legs. The opposite was true. She raised her knees to make herself more available.

She felt a sudden shock of cold. The chain was being fed into the moist heat of her vagina. A gasp caught her throat but she clutched frantically at the intruding chain with her trained vaginal muscles. Wolf's attentions had been prolonged and without release.

The change of action motivated Kroll and, almost before she had time to draw breath, a great sword of flesh was thrust between her softly parted lips. In her country it was a custom, in sexual play, for a man to spume into a woman's mouth, but it was not done through force but after much gentle preparation.

"Suck it, bitch," said Kroll. "Swallow me."

At the same moment, Wolf caressed her bud as well as pushing as much of the smooth body chain into her willing vagina as was possible. She felt her body convulse magnificently. It could not be stopped. It was just as it was when the noble took her virginity.

Mouth open, Zacora was able to engulf all of Kroll's hugeness. His tip moved into her gullet and this caressed it, soaking it with saliva. She could hear him groaning his pleasure and this increased her pleasure, making her climax repeat itself with double the strength.

The chain was pulled from her vagina, link by link, and she could feel the cushiony flesh clutching at the warmed metal, as if to keep it there. Suddenly, the chain was gone and her sex was clutching on the misty night air, grasping at nothing.

"Watch!" breathed Wolf to Brad and Pike. "Never have I seen such a welcome!"

The words made Zacora proud of the years of female training in Lokara; the learning how to love and be loved.

"Are you going to put it in?" asked Brad. He was the youngest of the sedan bearers and had no experience with women at all. He had never been given a chance to sink into the heat of a willing vessel. Wolf pushed him forward.

"You, my lad," he said laughing, "may take your turn, but be quick about it. My hunger is at least as great as yours."

Zacora felt smooth young thighs being pushed against hers, just as Kroll jerked deep into her throat. The first taste of his issue was thick and salty as though it was long stored in his huge sac. Jet after jet poured over her tongue and down into her gullet. Her training made it easy to take the rich liquid without gagging. It poured into her in a never ending stream.

There was a smooth jab at her slippery vaginal entrance. "That's it, lad," she heard Wolf say, "now press hard."

The penis which speared into her was long and thick, but it slid into her with very little resistance because she was so wet and ready. The cushiony walls caressed the young man's length, petting the smooth rigidity with skilful muscles. Brad was breathing hard.

The four men had treated her badly. Her buttocks still burned from the thrashing and her mind still reeled with their insults, but her training went so deep that she could not help herself. She had to pleasure Brad to the very best of her ability.

He drove into her, butting to the very limits of her womb. She, in turn, so far as her tethered arms would allow, gyrated under him, ignoring the stinging pain in her thrashed bottom. Her rear hole, still glowing from the attention of the willow twigs, pulsed in rhythm with her caressing vagina.

A final harsh breath signalled Kroll's climax had faded. The night air was free to blow across Zacora's fair features which had been so closely confined throughout his penetration of her mouth. He didn't stand immediately, but wiped his penis in her silky hair, leaving sticky streaks in the golden strands.

In the very depths of her vagina began a heaviness, a melting pot of pleasure which engulfed her and, in turn, the young man.

A mew of delight escaped Zacora's soft lips, lips which were silvery with the remains of Kroll's semen. She arched her back, craving Brad to take her body. He pounded her, holding the sharp arches of her slim hips to gain purchase, bruising her with the force of his grip.

"She's almost there, Brad," said Wolf excitedly, "And so are you. Fuck her! Fuck her hard!"

The crude language grated on Zacora's ears but, at the same time, it heightened her excitement. Her puff of silvery blonde hair upon her mound gyrated on the man's coarse black one, and this was another source of excitement. She felt him throb in her silky depths and she, automatically, squeezed with her well-trained muscles. He groaned, wetting her creamy body with the sweat of exertion, so that their skin squelched moistly as they moved.

He spurted into her. Time after time he spurted into her. The thrusts seemed never ending, but at last Wolf grabbed the lad's muscular shoulder, pulling him away from the helpless girl. Zacora saw Brad, panting and still making his emission a few yards away.

She felt hard hands on her strained shoulders. The pain made her wince, biting her soft lower lip. It was Wolf, the largest man, lowering himself into her. She saw his penis, so dark in the shadow of his own body as to look almost black.

Her entrance was fully open and drenched with Brad's sperm, but she tensed, trying to make her vessel tight for Wolf, trying to make it pamper him. He hovered above her, rough hands hard on her shoulders. He nudged at the warm wetness of her entrance with the rounded thickness of his globe. She could feel him opening her up, spreading the inner lips apart. Poised there, he looked down at her.

Prised open in this way, Zacora could feel Brad's hot liquid running from her; feel it seeping over the spread buttocks and down her splayed thighs. She had bent her knees and spread them outwards, making herself totally vulnerable for Wolf, wanting to please him.

"You are a used woman," he grunted cruelly in her face. His features were a mask of hatred; his need to hurt her naked form beneath him.

Zacora said nothing, but simply tried to ignore the pain in her shoulders. His grip was fierce on her soft flesh and her arms were becoming numb from their long confinement in one position above her head. She concentrated on the wonderful feelings in her sex. He penetrated her further, making the entrance slow and tantalising. She tilted her mound, offering a more open position.

Wolf's dark eyes slitted cruelly. "Surely," he hissed, "only a harlot would know such tricks." She saw him move his swarthy cheeks, gathering saliva and a great gob of his spit splashed on her pale cheek. He plunged into her fully, gyrating cruelly, and she met him movement for movement. It was an angry, frantic coupling with the sex skilled girl contracting her muscles around him, milking him of his sperm. His heavy balls smacked hard against her buttocks, already wet with Brad's spillage.

Another splash of liquid fell hotly on her swollen breasts. Wolf still held her at the shoulders, pinching the fine skin and bruising the delicate bones.

Zacora looked up, Pike was standing over them, his head thrown back, glorying in their sudden ascendancy over a woman. His penis was held in one hand, while the other was cupping his balls. His thick shaft was being manipulated vigorously and it was spurting in great hot splashes over her naked breasts.

She accepted her humiliation gladly. She smiled up at Wolf and was rewarded with another gob of saliva, aimed this time into her open soft lips. His movements were frantic, spearing his whole length into her. She could feel him pulsing and her own climax was so close, so very close.

CHAPTER FIVE

The new slave had arrived in a sedan chair, lying back on soft cushions. Naked, as a slave should be, she trembled in her chains as Megan peered into the curtained sedan. It was a delicious sound; the tinkling of the fine chains.

The nervous slave looked up at her new mistress with the biggest sapphire eyes Megan had ever seen. Long blonde curls - no, not truly blonde, gold, with streaks of silver - twisted over the pale shoulders to circle pert pink nipples. The breasts had the perfect roundness of youth. The skin was stretched over them drum-like and it swept down to a slender waist, so delicately curved that it asked to be caressed. Megan stretching out a finger and the slave flinched back into the cushions of the sedan.

The girl had a belly, a mere gentle swell from the dip of her navel. The nest! Oh, Megan had gasped at the sight of the nest. It pouted out, a pad of female flesh brushed with hair more silvery than that upon her lovely head. And the way she had been placed in the sedan by the guards made the silver-flecked labia part so that Megan could see the moist pink folds beneath. The nubbin, too, was plainly visible, achingly lovely, begging to be kissed by female lips.

The chains by which Zacora was held were light, but strong. The ankles were gripped by manacles, holding her shapely pale legs apart. The chain between the manacles was at full stretch, holding the legs taut. A well-placed padlock in each lower corner of the sedan pulled the ankles, and thus the full legs, wide apart.

The wrists, too, were shackled, but together. The arms were pulled high, Megan noticed, and fastened to the roof of the sedan, making the lovely breasts so taut that it looked as though the skin would burst.

A seemingly unnecessary chain was looped between ankles and wrists. It was very fine and, at intervals, were smooth round balls of different sizes. The placing of these devices, it seemed to Megan, was judged very precisely. There was one at the mouth, one between the deep valley of her breasts, one upon her sex mound and one, where the chain took a loose loop, at her sex entrance. Every slight movement caused the balls to give small stimulations, teasing almost.

Megan's mouth went dry at the sight presented to her, and her sex became puffy, more open, ready and wet. She had difficulty calling for the guards to unfasten the padlocks so the girl could be helped from the sedan.

As two guards stepped forward, presenting their hairy muscular buttocks as they bent into the curtained sedan, Megan had no desire to finger the leather thongs parting those delicious male clefts. Heavy sacs lay between the slightly parted thighs. Normally, Megan would not have been able to resist cupping these, caressing them, feeling them move within the loose skin. She did nothing except lick her lips, mentally running through the inventory of her sex toys. Which would be most appropriate to use on this sweet creature first? What would she use to train her to adore? Should she take her to tantalise her favourite customers? Yes, she decided, how they would love that extra stimulation.

Free and wobbly from long tethering in the sedan, Zacora stood beside Megan, head bowed in sad submission. Even in this position the breasts were taut and firm with sweet little nipples, gently tucked in, asking to be sucked to erection.

"Walk in front of me," ordered Megan.

Zacora's sapphire eyes looked up questioningly. Even with the looseness of the ankle chain, walking would not be easy.

"Do as I say!" Megan's voice was sharper. "And keep your head bowed."

The new captive took a tentative step towards the heavy wooden drawbridge. The girl was obviously nervous and unsure of herself.

Megan liked her new slaves to walk in front of her, so that she could admire their buttocks. Her eyes always strayed to that place. Those in front of her at that moment were particularly fine. The flesh was firm, sporting the most delightful slope down to the fullness at the lower margin. There was also an attractive parting at the bottom cleft which urged the viewer to want to investigate within those depths.

The sway was lovely too. Once the girl caught a rhythm, there was a swing of the flesh, pouting and parting, which was most provocative.

However, thought Megan, frowning, the girl, seemingly so pliant, also had a hint of rebelliousness. This must be beaten out of her. Her fingers itched as she mentally viewed the whip case. She lightly brushed the pads of her thumbs across those of her fingertips as if feeling the texture of different leather strips, how they would feel to her fingers before she striped the girl with them.

But she would be gentle in her discipline - at first. She lifted her eyes, dark and heavily outlined with black kohl, to look at the graceful length of the girl's body. Although pale there was a golden sheen as is found on a ripe fruit such as a peach. The skin begged to be caressed by mouth, fingers and lash.

The shoulders were wide for such a slender body and they were proud, for all the golden head was bent in submission. A strange mixture. This was no ordinary girl, that was plain enough.

"I'd better take you to the bath house and have you scrubbed." She wagged an admonishing finger. "Don't know what you've been up to with those guards."

Zacora said nothing. The guards were men and her strict training taught that they, even though they were servants of this woman, they must be protected and loved.

"Hm!" Megan sneered at her silence. "Four hulking guards carrying you in a sedan chair for five days and you did nothing? This I cannot believe. They would not be able to control themselves!" She laughed. "I know what those men are like. Couldn't resist a girl like you. I'll bet it was one after the other several times a day, every day."

Zacora remained silent.

Megan laughed even more loudly. "You were helpless," she reminded the girl. "In chains and your legs were splayed wide open." She gave a nod of understanding. "You allowed them to do it in your mouth, is that it? So their misbehaviour would not be discovered?"

Zacora hung her head in shame, blushing furiously.

"Nevertheless, I feel, so that I can discern the truth, I must inspect you," said Megan, "once we reach the bath house." Zacora had halted, her lustrous golden tresses hanging loosely from the crown of her head and over the lovely curves of her breasts. "Not far now."

The girl shuffled forward, for her ankles were becoming sore with the chafing of the manacles. Megan loved the way her arms were held loosely in front of her, hands at the soft warmth of the silver nest. The length of chain looped from ankles to wrists brushed the satin skin of the inner thighs in a most stimulating manner. Megan could feel her own sap gathering between swollen lips and her nubbin jutting quite urgently between her uncovered cleft.

"Here we are," said Megan cheerfully, swinging open an oak door. "This is the bath house."

Zacora hung back, for the echoing marble chamber was full of giggling girls. "Here is the new girl." Megan pushed the reluctant captive into the dimly lit, steam-filled room, and spoke in an almost motherly fashion. "I'm going to inspect her, if you would like to watch, my dears. I fear she has been very naughty with the guards."

Cries of 'oooh' and 'aaah' went up from the naked girls.

"You two!" Megan pointed to two well-built young ladies drying themselves at the edge of one of the round marble tubs sunk into the stone floor.

The girls looked at each other, giggling that they had been chosen, then turned to Megan to question their task.

"Get her up on the examining table, but I want the chains undisturbed." Megan looked eager, her dark eyes bright and her scarlet lips slightly parted and moist.

The fairer of the two girls looped her strong hands under Zacora's armpits, while the darker one lifted her at bent knees. "She's very light, mistress," said the dark one, placing the new captive on the bench. Smiling at Zacora she splayed her knees and carefully put the shackled feet together. This had the effect of opening up the sex lips quite nicely.

Zacora looked down and, seeing how she was spread, she blushed in humiliation. She tried to close her knees, but Megan quickly stepped forward, slapping them wide again. "And keep them that way," she ordered.

Other girls were gathering eagerly around the bench. One even stroked the underswell of each breast, watching how each inverted nipple sprang out almost immediately.

"She's very sensitive, mistress," remarked the girl, smiling down at the blushing Zacora.

"And so will you be," said Megan sharply, "if you don't leave her alone. She's not for you to touch."

In her hand, Megan held an instrument. Before using this she spread the soft sex leaves open with her fingers, as if gaging the width to which they would open. Immediately, she saw the girl's clitoris jerk to attention. It was stiff, peachy coloured and shiny with moisture. Zacora was indeed sensitive.

"How pretty!" she couldn't help murmuring, stretching out a gentle finger to stroke the jutting erection of the bud.

Megan lowered her head and placed a wide syringe into the pulsing entrance. Yes, it was pulsing. It wanted something to go in. The skin was smooth, so moist and silky. It was made to be penetrated.

"I am going to take a sample of the fluid within you," Megan told the suffering girl. "To discern just how much the guards defiled you."

Zacora shuddered, hoping that the guards seed had drained away. Megan looked at her suspiciously.

"Hm, we'll see," she said quietly.

The syringe was as thick as a medium cockshaft. It was smooth and slid in easily. Megan knew that the girl would feel a mild sucking sensation and, maybe a sense of fullness. She watched the dainty bottom cheeks lift a little from the bench, as if wanting more. The mistress removed the syringe and held it to the light to check the contents.

"Milky looking," she noted, "quite copious. I really cannot believe that this is all your own. No woman produces so much lubrication - not even me."

The girls gathered, so close to the bench, sniggering. One or two of them received hard slaps for their pains.

Zacora, almost in tears, held her guilty secret silently.

Megan shrugged. "What matter anyway, I shall still have you scrubbed to make sure. I have very intimate plans for you."

Spirits sagging, Zacora allowed herself to be lifted from the bench. All the girls seemed very eager to be the ones to scrub.

Still chained, the captive was slipped into one of the deep tubs. The water was pleasantly hot and aromatically perfumed. Megan watched as her prize was shampooed; her long golden curls floating out like a living fan upon the swirling water. She watched as the girls scrubbed under, over and around the sensitive mounds of the breasts, until they glowed scarlet. She watched as many willing hands dipped down to finger the silvery mound, and into the slit. She heard a slight moan as a sensitive spot was teased. It was going to be sheer delight playing with this young woman. She looked so innocent and yet she was receptive. It wasn't often one found both qualities in a slave.

"Take her out," she ordered. Her voice was quite husky with longing and she found herself lifting her black clingy dress and stroking her plump mound. She stopped, just in time. It wasn't good for discipline to do such things in front of the slaves. They were the ones to be done to, after all, not to do.

The captive was pampered as she was dried with soft cloths. All the girls took a part of her and rubbed and patted her dry. Zacora loved it when her pale skin flushed with embarrassment as the girls reached the most intimate parts. It was quite amazing how, though embarrassed, her nipples popped out as hard pegs and her nether lips became inflamed and swollen.

"You can all bring her to my play room as a special treat," said Megan, "but you will have to leave when I begin my games."

An excited twittering set up among the girls. Some of them were still glowing from their bath and all were still. Their young bodies shone with moisture and nipples of every shape and shade dripped enticingly, and in the midst of them was the trembling figure of the new captive.

The other girls were long trained slaves, quite happy in their role. Megan looked at Zacora, being pulled by her body chain by several girls. She looked sad though her body glowed prettily from the treatment she had just received.

Hands stroked Zacora's nakedness, infiltrating her front and rear clefts. Megan saw her, surreptitiously, bear down on the fingers, urging deeper penetration. Oh, she thought, I can't wait to begin on her.

The procession of women, chattering and giggling, made its way to the vast chamber where all new slaves were taught the Meleagan way, "Where do you come from?" whispered one little creature in Zacora's ear.

"Lokara," replied Zacora, "we were trained to please men - but not women."

"No more talking, you girls." Megan heard her own voice. It was sharp and edgey.

They all entered the play room, Zacora in the middle of the crowd. I should be excited, thought Megan, by having all my girls around me, fresh and clean from the bath house. But she wanted the beautiful Zacora on her own.

"Go away now," she said. Her voice was softer, huskier.

When they were alone she turned to look at Zacora, smiling lasciviously. Taking the hem of her black dress she lifted it and pulled it over her head, Her full figure was naked apart from a narrow red suspender belt, black stockings and tight ankle boots with heels.

"What do you think of me?" she asked, pirouetting and posing her heavy breasts and pillows of flesh forming her bottom.

Zacora, head bowed, was silent.

Megan strode towards her crossly to drag her to a pillar at the centre of the room, hooking her wrist chain to a high placed hook. She grinned as she saw the tight breasts lift with the tension. In a vertical position, the body chain was much tighter and the smooth balls fitted into their appointed places: mouth, breast valley, silver mound and the sex slit.

Megan stood back looking at her new slave. "Very nice indeed. How do these little teasers feel?" She rubbed the balls at the mound and slit, grinning as she saw Zacora wriggle and bear down on the titillation.

"Something more fleshy is called for," said Megan, stroking at her own dark brown forest, spreading the swiftly swelling lips to bare her moist nubbin. "Look up, my pet, and you'll see what I mean."

Obediently, Zacora raised her sad eyes and they widened at what she saw. Depicted on the high ceiling was the Garden of Eden. Adam watched in horror as the serpent coiled around Eve's leg, although she was obviously ecstatic. Her mouth was open and eyes glazed in lust. The head of the serpent was poised at her dripping entrance.

When Zacora attempted to lower her head she found that she could not. Megan had plaited her hair into a loop and fixed it firmly to the post by some means.

Megan went to a cabinet, leaving Zacora forced to stare at the defilement of Eve. The girl was trembling, Megan knew, for she could hear the slight tinkle of the chains, metal upon metal. She smiled to herself, allowing the girl to think that she was to be penetrated by a live snake. "It isn't poisonous," Megan said calmly, "and it absolutely loves warm, dark places. And snakes aren't slimy, you know, not at all. Not a bit like people think, so you'd better set to and create some of that famous sap of yours."

"Please, mistress," whimpered Zacora. "I hate snakes. Anything but that."

Megan laughed. "Oh, I have lots of treats in store for you," she assured. "Lots of playthings, but I want you to feel the glorious wriggliness of my little pet first." She turned to look at her slave, smiling a little as she looked at the forcibly held silver head, the pale arms stretched high to lift the breast mounds, the long legs balanced on tip toe and manacled around the broad pole. Megan felt light headed at the sight; almost drunk.

In the cabinet, the cupboard she called her toy box, there was a wide variety of smooth carved lengths of wood, dildoes, worn with frequent usage, of every shape and size imaginable.

Slowly, she sorted through the collection, looking for the special one. It wasn't a real snake, but her wood carver had made a fine job of creating a dildo replica of the reptile. It was made in segments to give the impression of movement when Megan pulled a cord at the tail. There was even a tiny forked tongue which could be retracted when the carved serpent was inserted. Even the colours were realistic upon the scale-like marking.

A wicked smile wreathed Megan's round face as she took it from the cabinet, holding it on the flat of both palms as she swung her plump near-naked body across the room to Zacora's bound one. "Here he is, the little beauty," she said proudly. "Not so little really. I hope you're feeling nice and open because his girth is quite huge." She giggled. "Just eaten, you see." The giggle came again at the lie.

She held up the smoothly carved snake, surreptitiously pulling the tiny cord so that the serpent waved slowly on the upheld palms. It was kept below Zacora's eye line, so that the view of it was just sufficient to give the impression of live movement. Megan was delighted when she saw the girl flinch in terror.

"Come now," the woman cajoled. "It's like cold water - it really isn't so bad once you're in." She paused, thinking. "Or rather, perhaps I should say, once it's in."

Zacora's whole body was taut with fear, flinching back against the post. Her eyes were closed against the awful scene on the ceiling above her, and yet her sex pouch was ready for something to stretch the soft cushiony walls.

Not a snake though! Oh no, not a snake!

"Here he comes!" Megan made the snake wriggle, made the forked tongue tickle the swollen silver lips one last time before she retracted it. She brushed her own plump body, her belly and her cushiony breasts against Zacora's willowy one and positioned the snake head at the girl's entrance. She pushed it forward, smiling as she heard the whisper of horror change to a sigh of delight as the wriggling thickness entered and stretched the soft, moist membranes.

"You see! I told you!" Megan was triumphant. She brushed her huge pillows of soft flesh across Zacora's firm tight breasts as she eased the plumpness of the snake replica into the receptive moistness of the girl's sex passage. She could feel the captive's young muscles pulsing around the wriggling intrusion and the breathing was one of excitement; the excitement of a sensation. Megan pulled the cord, very gently, and a groan escaped the girl, becoming louder as the intrusion became deeper and more vibrant.

"See how your pleasure flows over my little pet," she said huskily. "Your nubbin tip rubs beautifully over his tail and he delights upon the liquid which you pour over him." Megan sniffed the air. "Oh yes, he loves your fresh musky aroma. Once more, my precious little slave, but we shall place him into your rear passage now that you have wetted him so nicely with your love sap."

Very slowly, the snake-like dildo was withdrawn from the pulsing sex pouch.

"No, mistress, please," pleaded Zacora. There was humiliation in her begging, but Megan took no notice. "Not there, please!"

Unheeding, Megan released her new captive. The girl's legs were weak from the strong orgasms given by the dildo and she fell gracefully in a heap to the floor.

"Good," smiled Megan. "We'll keep the thighs open and your bottom just clear of the ground." Zacora's legs were placed in this position around the post, still using the ankle manacles and chain.

Keeping the dildo out of sight, so the illusion of the snake was kept, Megan played with the climax-relaxed body. She kissed the lifted moistness between the splayed thighs, sniffing the aroma as she nuzzled into the wetness with her nose. She kissed each breast, misted with the heat of orgasm, swollen to tenderness. She kissed the soft, parted lips, transferring the girl's own juices into her mouth. The captive was so excited that there was no hint of embarrassment or humiliation. Megan frowned. She missed those things in a girl. Surely, innocence could not be peaked away so quickly by climaxes?

"I'll soon fix you," she said hoarsely. "He's entering you now. You've made him nice and slippery, so there should not be too much pain."

Zacora's sapphire blue eyes flashed open. It was as if she had been mesmerised by that first orgasm from the snake, and now she was back to reality. "That's better," said Megan cheerfully. She pressed the pale lifted bottom cheeks to expose the rear mouth and pull it open. The snake head poked at the tight wrinkled opening. The girl shuddered, but it wasn't clear whether it was a shiver of horror or of delight. Megan shrugged, probably delight, for she was massaging the fully exposed nubbin. The dildo snake moved as she pulled the cord and inched into the darkness of the rear passage. The girl was breathing quickly and rhythmically in her bonds.

Megan was delighted to note that Zacora kept her hands stretched high above her head. The girl certainly knew her place, knew that she should be passive and pliant. The flexible dildo was high up within her now and Megan was stroking the nubbin with all of her moistened fingers. The hoarse breathing was quicker, more urgent, and there was a bearing down on the snake.

"Let your full pleasure flow, my lovely," Megan urged. "I have to teach you every nuance of sensuality and you are such a good pupil."

With strong pulsations in the young muscles the snake was gradually eased out of the rear mouth. The girl lay passive, her moist silver sex purse open and the swollen lips fluttering. The nubbin jerked in and out of the pink leaves, throbbing with its recent satisfaction. Fluid, pearly and warm, oozed from the darkness of the pouch. Tears flowed down the pale cheeks as Zacora lay, still chained with her legs humiliatingly parted.

"Tears, my darling?" Megan questioned. "Why so, when my little pet has cossetted you so nicely?"

"Please let me go," begged Zacora.

"Aren't you enjoying yourself with our little games?" Megan raised a quirky eyebrow and squatted before the girl, displaying herself lewdly.

"No - yes," she stammered. "Oh, I don't know what I mean."

Megan watched the girl eagerly, seeing what effect her display might produce. The sapphire eyes focused on the dark lushness of Megan's sex pouch, open and slick with creamy lubrication. The young lips seemed to open automatically and the tongue protruded ready to tease an opening or a jutting bud. Shuffling eagerly, Megan moved towards the beckoning, fully open slit. There was a warm, molten heaviness in her belly. She felt that she could hardly breath for the excitement.

The spell was broken by the door to the chamber opening. Angrily, Megan turned on the intruder. It was her brother Gareth, his small thin body dressed only in a square of leather, such was worn by the guards and other male slaves. His large cock was far too big to be covered by the square of leather and it hung, in an detumescent state, several inches below the loincloth.

"Want any help?" His eyes fluttered hungrily as he looked at the prone girl with her buttocks lifted and her legs splayed around the pillar. "She is lovely, isn't she?"

"And she's mine," spat Megan. "Harold bought her for me."

"Yes, but surely I can have a turn," pouted Gareth. His cock was rising, thick and long, lifting the black loincloth.

Megan cocked her head on one side, giving the matter some thought. "Very well then," she conceded. "After dinner, we'll get the whips out. I'll get the servants to feed her."

Megan gave a last lingering look at Zacora. She was born to be a sexual plaything, a toy for the joy of men - and women. The sweet pliant face was so soft and seemed to wait to be abused. Those seductive lips were always parted as if waiting to suck a man's shaft. And that flowing hair, streaked with gold and silver, cascading to the waist, over the creamy shoulders and tantalising the lovely breasts!

The neatly trimmed triangle at the top of the thighs waited to be penetrated by dildoes and cocks alike. The firm, plump lips seemed always to be parted, at the ready to be intruded. The silver fronds were always delicately dewed.

CHAPTER SIX

Immediately after dinner Megan and her son Gareth returned to the play room, their eager eyes darting to the lovely vision.

There was an empty dish and a wine goblet at the foot of the pillar where the girl was chained. Her hands were high above her head and her legs splayed backwards around the pillar.

"I wonder if it hurts," said Gareth. He fumbled under his loincloth, feeling his growing thickness.

"I don't know," Megan said testily, "ask her." She was busy choosing more of her toys from the cabinet: a slim narrow paddle, a broad strap, a drumstick with a particularly bulbus end and a fine leather lash.

Gareth looked at Zacora's freshly brushed hair, tended, no doubt, by the maid who brought the girl her food. "You have lovely hair," he murmured, letting it shimmer through his fingers. The slave said nothing, simply looked at him sadly and mutely. His fingers strayed to the pinkness of the captive's nipples, tweaking them to sharp erection. He smiled as he saw her wince, but he also saw a twitch of the silver haired love lips. Perhaps, he thought, it wasn't hurting her after all, but he asked her again. "Does it hurt, being balanced on tip toe like that?"

"My arms hurt," she said.

"Is that all?" He sounded almost disappointed. "Doesn't it hurt here?" He touched the softness of her sex pouch, stroking the puffy silver mound and then the stretched out lips. "I should have thought it would, being held up like that."

Zacora lowered her lashes, embarrassed at his touch. This urged Gareth on and his loincloth was held high by the sudden rise of his cock. He prodded deeper into her pouch, enjoying the silky wetness.

"Do you mind me feeling her like this?" he asked. His sister was so much larger than he was and had such a filthy temper.

"I'm being patient with you," Megan said softly, "like Harold told me to be. I'm going to use lots of toys on her when you've had her. Just make her nice and wet and slippery."

Gareth's eyes sparkled. "Fetch the standing box," he begged. His stature was such that he needed extra height in order to penetrate the girl, any girl.

The box brought the tip of his gleaming erection to just the correct height to place it in the moist entrance. Zacora smiled sweetly at him. The smile made him melt inside, made the stretched fineness of his end globe feel that it would burst. Blindly he probed the thickness at the soft warmth of her entrance. There was slight resistance to his massiveness, but suddenly they were coupled together. Her willingness made him all the more enthusiastic, and he pounded into her rhythmically.

An outside force on a particularly hard inward thrust made Gareth grunt with the sharp pain in his naked buttocks. The pain came again, sharper this time, harder. Suddenly, the pain became pleasure. He felt himself jetting his spume into the slave's pulsing sex pouch.

"How did you like it?" He heard Megan's voice through the mist of his orgasm. "Did it enhance your pleasure?"

Zacora was bemused by her strange masters. All her life her teaching was to be obedient, to give pleasure and to be subservient. She was so willing to please the right man. Where was he?

Megan shrugged. "Get her down for me and put her over the whipping saddle." Gareth saw Zacora's eyes widen fearfully.

Gareth caressed Zacora's body, feeling the silky smoothness, soon to be discovered by the whip. His penis had descended into limpness but began to rise again. He was gentle in loosening Zacora's chains, making sure that he brushed his moist globe over every part of her naked skin which presented itself.

"Over she goes," said Megan. "I think she is now sufficiently used to being chained to realise that we are her masters."

Gareth nodded again. His eyes were fixed on the pale naked buttocks which were posed delicately over the whipping saddle. The legs were splayed wide so that he could see the girl's open sex pouch. Her firm breasts were pressed into the tanned and polished leather. The saddle was balanced on a waist high platform, keeping the victim at a comfortable height for discipline.

Balanced over the whipping saddle, Zacora could feel the cold, smooth leather massaging her hot skin. She saw her hair fall in a shimmering cascade of gold and silver to the floor and waited patiently for the next stage of discipline.

"How do you enjoy our little game so far?" questioned Megan, as if reading her thoughts.

Zacora was silent for a moment, choosing her words carefully, so as not to anger those strange people. Their discipline was given as an end in itself. Her training in Lokara was always to bring pleasure to men and, therefore, to herself. "You must do as you think fit, mistress," she said politely.

Gareth was delving his penis into the very depths of the shimmering tresses, slicking his bursting globe through its silkiness. Zacora saw a droplet of his seed run down a golden strand, hanging there like a pearl.

"Oh, I will," chuckled Megan, "have no fear on that account." She was weighing the thin paddle of wood in one hand and the thick leather strap in the other, flicking them on her palms, testing their feel on her own skin.

Zacora felt her stroke the paddle over the creamy hillocks of her buttocks, so lifted by the whipping saddle. She felt her skin tremble, flutter involuntarily at the touch. The two tormentors had her completely at their mercy. She felt so helpless and vulnerable to them. This very feeling excited her sex, making it pout, even though she despised them.

Humiliation was part of her training in Lokara, but not like this. She felt Gareth stroke her offered body and she groaned piteously. He pulled the chains which held her, tugging sharply on the manacles and chafing her slim wrists and ankles.

"The strap," Megan decided. The strap was a thick length of leather, composed of several layers bonded together. Zacora saw Megan flex it and couldn't prevent a deep shiver of fear. "This little beauty," Megan told her, "becomes hard and inflexible from lack of use, but lucky for you Uncle Harold has bought several new girls in recent weeks, so it is nice and flexible." She chuckled happily.

Uncle Harold, thought Zacora. That must be the strong handsome man in the carriage at the auction. Discipline with him would be joy, she mused sadly. How she would please him!

"Let me do it," begged Gareth, reaching out for the strap.

"We'll both do it." said Megan. "Strap and paddle together. You'll enjoy that, won't you?" The thick leather was edged into the splayed cleft of Zacora's buttocks.

"Yes, mistress," agreed the captive obediently.

"That's settled then," said Megan, a cruel edge to her voice. "You take the paddle, Gareth, and I'll use the strap."

Zacora felt her legs being pulled yet further apart and a smooth wedge placed in the bottom cleft to fully reveal the rear entrance.

"Ready?" Megan asked, holding the thick strap high above the left buttock cheek.

Gareth murmured his readiness and both instruments struck at the same time. The pains were so different, one much sharper than the other. Zacora felt her flesh begin to glow in that familiar way and shudder under the force of the blows. She allowed herself only a very small muted murmur and this was muffled by the thick curtain of golden hair.

"The new ones usually make much more noise than that," said Megan. She sounded disappointed. "Again," she ordered.

The paddle and strap beat down again. The girl knew that her pale flesh would be flushed in vertical welts. She murmured again, but this time, not from pain, but embarrassment. The stimulation was causing a gentle pulsing of her fully revealed rear bud. Her excitement was becoming very evident.

"Harder!" snarled Megan. "Harder!"

Zacora knew that the woman was aware of her enjoyment. She must concentrate harder on dislike.

The paddle struck down. The leather strap striped the pert cheeks twice, very quickly.

Zacora's vulnerable bottom wriggled. She was trying hard not to show the strange pleasure she was finding in the cruelty, but perhaps her early training went too deep.

"Just one moment," ordered Megan. Zacora felt the smoothness of the paddle laid flat against her puffy open sex lips. It was stroked back and forth between the fully spread portals and the girl felt her face flush as the erect pinkness of the nubbin was grazed by the invading instrument.

"Look!" squealed Megan crossly, obviously holding the paddle for Gareth to see. "It is soaked with her juices. She's excited."

"Some more punishment?" Her brother sounded hopeful and very excited.

"But what?" Megan sounded very angry. She felt that slaves should collapse in floods of tears when they were brought to her. Only then would they know their place and behave obediently. She stroked Zacora's fiery skin with the paddle, soothing the mounds with the girl's copious juices. She stood behind her, brushing her dark bush against the parted cheeks, caressing the open-ness of the cleft.

"How does it feel, my dear?" she whispered into the heavy fall of golden hair. Zacora sighed a breath. The hair was lifted so that Megan could see the girl's embarrassed and humiliated face. How Zacora longed for that unique combination of love and humiliation. But that was behind her, in Lokara. Here there was no love, only punishment.

Zacora's eyes became expressionless. Her finely sculpted face remained passive. It looked neither sad nor excited. Only her mouth, with its lovely wide moist lips, told of her true feelings. They were lightly parted and the tip of the pink tongue protruded, shiny and moving ever so slightly. It told of hidden pleasure; hidden delight in her treatment. The delight would be so much greater if the punishments were done by the right person. The strong one. What did the sedan bearer call him? Harold the Pretender? Pretender of what, Zacora wondered.

CHAPTER SEVEN

"I have an idea," said Megan brightly. "Have you ever worked in a kitchen, my dear?"

The endearment was false, Zacora knew, and she shook her head. "My training is to pleasure men of noble birth, for I myself am such."

Megan gave a snort of disbelief. "That's as maybe," she said carefully. "Well, I think a spell in the kitchen might knock such stupid ideas from your head."

"I agree," said Gareth. "Are we going to dress her?" The question was asked softly as if the lad hoped that the answer would be negative.

A finger tapped Megan's lips as she thought. Finally, she shook her head. "Let's take her down just as she is. She'll enjoy doing kitchen tasks with her body free of the encumbrance of clothes."

"Must I wear clothes?" Gareth stroked the silky erection peeping hugely and coyly from his loincloth.

"Certainly, you must," Megan said crossly. "We cannot demean ourselves in front of the servants."

Zacora felt Megan's hands stroking the broad welts which stood proud from the rest of the flesh. The girl knew that the woman was admiring her handiwork and watching the fine silk flutter at her touch. "Hm," she murmured. "Delicious, and you enjoyed it, didn't you, my precious?" Zacora shuddered at the false endearment. "Don't shake your head for I know that you did."

Brother and sister dressed hurriedly. Zacora was looped pliantly over the whipping saddle, awaiting the next command.

"Get up!" The command was snapped as Megan smoothed her short silky dress. It lay tightly on her plump frame, pulling across her breast pillows and skimming the hillocks of her bottom. She looked scathingly at Gareth.

He was wearing a loose white shirt. Over this was a hunting green jerkin, belted at the waist and reaching the top of his slim thighs. His largest attribute lay long and thick, nestling under his hose. His thin face was eager as he prepared to follow Megan.

"Go!" said Megan, pushing Zacora in front of her.

The girl knew that her scarlet beaten buttocks were being examined as they walked. She was conscious of the silver trails of Gareth's spume coating her legs as it ran down the peachy skin.

"What shall we do in the kitchen?" asked Gareth.

"Nothing." Megan smacked Gareth's lank hair and grimaced at the grease. "We just give orders and make other people work."

"Oh." Zacora heard disappointment in Gareth's voice. His chill hands were testing the perfect peach halves of her buttocks, flushed to delicate ripeness by the beating.

There was a smacking sound, solid and somehow pleasantly comforting. Megan was slapping her own thigh with a long lash chosen earlier. In her other hand she held a drumstick with a beautifully smooth globe, large like a good sized orange.

Zacora swept an anxious glance over her satin-smooth shoulder. Both Megan and Gareth grinned cruelly at her, waving the implements tantalisingly. The girl bowed her head, shuffling a little in the awkward chains. Her long pale hands were clasped together, the thumbs brushing the silver, fluffy nest. Megan, skipping along in front, watched the movement.

"Oh, do it more, dear," she urged, "Slip both thumbs into the sweetness of the cleft. Stroke your own slipperiness up and down and graze the tip."

Zacora looked up at the woman. All the girls in her class in Lokara were taught about self-pleasure, but it was for the entertainment of their husbands or future husbands; to be done in the privacy of the bedchamber not in some public place for all to see.

"I was taught that it is wrong."

"Never mind all that nonsense. Do as you are told. Entertain us as we walk to the kitchens."

Gareth joined Megan, having feasted his eyes to the full of the swollen redness of the well-disciplined bottom. "Yes, do it," he urged, his sex sword massively thick under his stretched hose. His hands rubbed urgently at the monstrous swelling and Zacora saw his eyes glint excitedly as her thumbs trembled at the silver mound. Tears glazed her deep blue eyes and her whole body trembled with the depth of her embarrassment.

Her face flushed to a delicate rose, Zacora tentatively slipped both thumbs between already swollen outer petals. She looked at the two watchers through thick fluttering lashes, as if to ask if she was going about the task correctly. They nodded avidly.

"Open those little sweeties up," Megan urged. The tip of her lash touched the silver fronded pouting outer lips.

The blush grew deeper, but she did as she was bid. The two watchers walked backwards, not wanting to miss a moment, their eyes focused downwards. With thumbs only, Zacora peeled the lips right back, revealing a sex bud which was scarlet and jutting from the tiny hood. A new feeling swept over her. The humiliation was replaced by pride and she walked with her pubis thrust forward, neat but plump.

Gareth groaned, leaning forward to look more closely. He could still see a pearly ring of his foamy seed gathered at her open, obviously willing, entrance.

"Use your middle finger to rub that lovely nubbin," ordered Megan. She prodded the shining scarlet bud of flesh with her lash, loving it when the girl shuddered at the stroking touch.

Their progress to the kitchen was slower now, for all three were engrossed in what was going on in the girl's sex pouch. A slender dexterous finger was flickering up and down each side of the slippery shaft. The silver fluff of the pubis seemed to puff outwards like a peacock's chest. The swollen lips were firmly held back by obedient thumbs. The loose chains from wrists to ankles grazed the long legs as the girl walked, tantalising herself. The movement of the chain made the action more sensual, more slave-like.

Suddenly, the arch of the slender back became more pronounced and a husky whimper was drawn from the girl. The silver fronded pubis jerked and she pulled fiercely on the plump lips with her thumbs.

"Beautiful!" whispered Megan. "Take the middle finger away to show us how it jerks." There was the splendid nubbin, swollen to twice the normal size and glowing with heat. It danced on the moist flush of the silky sex bud, pulsing with energy. The tip jerked out from the hood, looking almost angry as well as joyful. Megan could not resist giving it a playful flick with the very tip of the lash.

Gareth was panting and his sex sword throbbed in his hose. He reached out to the still open sex pouch, feeling the heat and generous streaming of moisture produced by the girl. "We've never had one as willing, Megan," he said hoarsely. "She's the one that Harold has been looking for all these years, isn't she?"

"She's what we've all been looking for," said Megan wistfully.

The heat from the kitchen seeped from the partially open door and there was the spitting sound of a large piece of meat being cooked on a spit. There were voices, one man's voice raised in anger and several girls laughing and chattering.

Megan flung open the heavy door and her large presence was sufficient to stop the noise. The chief cook, like all the male servants, wore only the small loincloth. He was busy smacking a maid servant, thrown across his knee, her many frilled coarse petticoats drawn to her waist. Her chubby naked bottom glowed with the friction created by his hands and the tremendous heat from the huge kitchen range.

"Problems?" asked Megan, pushing Zacora before her. Her blonde head hung low, allowing the silvery curtain to sway about her oval face.

"The usual," said the cook. He pushed the little maid from his lap and stood, tall and proud. He was looking eagerly in Zacora's direction. "This young madam," he said, prodding the toe of his soft leather boot on the reddened bottom of the maid, "fancied giving herself a little pleasure with one of the master's carrots."

Gareth gaped; his eyes wide with lust. "Is it still there?" He turned the maid over, revealing her lush dark brown thatch. Disappointment was patently obvious on his thin face to find that no root vegetable protruded.

"Is this a new girl?" The chef reached out, feeling the firm flesh of Zacora's breasts, testing their weight and meatiness. He turned her round, cupping the cheeks of her buttocks. He made Zacora feel that she was so much meat being tested for roasting. "She must have clothing or she may be damaged." He gave her another sharp perusal. "I'm surprised you wish her to work in the kitchen. She is such a beauty I should have thought that she would be more suitable for the bedchamber - for Harold."

"We're giving her lots of tests," piped up Gareth, "and one of them is to be in the kitchen. There are so many varieties of toys in kitchens, are there not?"

The chef smiled. "Indeed there are, young master."

Megan tutted in annoyance. "We're wasting time. I still have my lash to use and my drumstick." She looked around. "May I use your milking stool, chef?"

"Of course, mistress."

Megan moved the milking stool close to the range with the blazing fire and the turning spit. "Kneel over this," she ordered Zacora, "and make sure that your breasts are nicely separated over the stool."

Zacora knelt by the fire. Heat blasted from the cooking fire and she could feel her pale skin flush and sweat break out in tiny pearly beads on her naked skin. Submissively, she swept her long arms behind her and wriggled slightly to position her breasts as Megan required.

"Bottom raised, if you please," Megan said crisply.

The heat was unbearable and Zacora looked up at her tormentors, pleading for a cooler place to receive further beatings, for she was sure that was to be her fate.

"Now, now," chided Megan. "This will not do." She placed firm hands on the arches of Zacora's hips and lifted the full buttocks high. She cossetted each breast very precisely on each side of the stool, patting them lightly as if they were soft scoops of butter, fresh from the churn. Firm hand on the tumbled softness of the golden hair, she forced the girl's head down to the stone floor.

She watched Zacora flinch, waiting for further blows. "Shuffle your knees apart, thighs wide," Megan ordered.

The girl's body was gleaming with sweat; slick with it. Silvery streams joined and flickered in the dancing light of the huge fire.

Tendrils of hair, soaked now with sweat, sprang into tight curls around her oval face. Her body glowed as though every inch had taken severe punishment, but, obedient and pliant as ever, she remained as she had been placed.

Megan rolled her smooth wooden drumstick along the hollow of the captive's back, wetting it in the pools of perspiration gathered in the hollow between shoulders and buttocks. She placed the polished globe at the entrance of the girl's body. This was slick with a slippery mixture of sweat and love sap. Megan played the globe between the wet silvery lips, feeling how these clutched tenderly at the intrusion.

The kitchen staff gathered to watch the diversion and seemed not to mind the severe heat blasting from the fire. "Lift further, my dear," Megan urged. "Let your admirers see how prettily your pouch opens for an audience."

Zacora, humiliated though she was, arched her buttocks as high as they would go, knowing that she would love the swirling sensation of a watched orgasm. She could feel her nubbin pressing hard against the drumstick, delighting in the polished smoothness. Suddenly, the wooden globe was pressed forward by Megan and Zacora gasped at the sudden thick intrusion. It was what was needed to bring her to her climax

The assembled audience gasped as they watched the large globe enter the gaping, milky gateway and the glowing, erect nubbin jerk ecstatically on the polished stick.

"Shall I remove it?" asked Gareth, reaching forward.

"No!" said Megan sharply. "I wish it to be left in for the next stage."

Gareth stroked the girl's glowing body. "She's burning," he said.

Megan shrugged. "So am I." She ran her sweating hands down her black dress, clinging tightly to her ample curves. She took the long thin lash from the top of her stocking, where she had placed it to leave her hands free. It made a sharp crack as she tested it upon the stone floor. The kitchen staff stepped back, not wishing to be in the path of the lash when it was cracked again.

The finely cut leather whipped across the splayed buttocks and the girl murmured softly. It wasn't a moan of pain, for the bulbous drumstick was still inserted. It was a moan of strange pleasure, hissed out between clenched teeth.

"Again," hissed the chef. "Let us see you measure her buttocks with the lash again."

The spread bottom tensed, ready for another lash of pain. Zacora could feel her breasts, one each side of the stool, become tender and swollen with the surfeit of desire. Hot liquid took slow streams along the deeply inserted drumstick and she knew that she presented a most lewd sight. Somehow this thought made the molten heaviness in her belly all the greater.

The lash snaked around her tender body; first from one side and then the other. The thin strip of leather was becoming wet as it soaked up the salty fluid of Zacora's sweat.

Light-headed and satiated, she softly murmured that her orgasms were many. The stone floor around the stool was dark with a mixture of fluids. Her golden hair was saturated, falling in many tiny ringlets around her.

"Enough," said Megan.

The kitchen workers fell back, returning to their tasks. The chef stared down at the girl, gleaming and shining in the firelight; stared down at the buttocks striated with fine red lines; stared dawn at the polished intrusion in the liquid heat of the sex pouch. His climaxes had come fast and furious as he watched the lashing and he too was now satiated.

Gareth could not restrain himself. In watching the lovely Zacora take her discipline, he found it necessary to seek out the kitchen maid. Petticoats swished high over her head, he flung her face down upon the scrubbed deal table and took her from the rear. To mimic Zacora he made the pretty little buttocks hotly inflamed with the flat of his palm before spreading them to their limit.

The female entrance of the maid was creamily lubricated, open and ready and Gareth plunged in with gusto. She wriggled her bottom, which encouraged him to go in to the hilt. He could feel her cushiony flesh stretch with his wide girth and he could feel his male sword pulsing, almost before he was fully inserted. His spume gushed before he was ready. He tried to prevent it, by pulling back from the warm pouch. Nevertheless, it fountained over the burning skin stretched so tightly across the proud hillocks.

At this juncture, Zacora was still receiving the light flicking of the thin whip and within moments Gareth was erect again. Using his own hot seed, he massaged the struggling maid's rear entrance, opening it up first with one finger, then two and then three. She was bearing down her lovely bottom, which urged him to intrude into the tight little hole. She moaned loudly, especially when he reached around her to spread her nether lips and tickled her nubbin.

At last, Zacora, still chained, was taken from the kitchen and given a place to sleep. It was a narrow cot, to which she was tightly tethered, her wrists stretched high above her head and ankles pulled wide to each side of the iron frame. A rough blanket was thrown over her to keep out the cold, but it also served to irritate her punished, tender skin.

She lay awake for many hours in her discomfort, but in those sleepless hours she thought about the strength of the man she saw in the carriage; his smile, confident and powerful, He was the man she wished to pleasure for the rest of her life.

But she did not know him. He might be cruel, like this evil Aunt of his and her repugnant son, wishing to inflict pain without the pleasure of love.

Her mind flashed back to the jailer and she shuddered at his crudeness, but she must admit that he gave her pleasure.

The sedan bearers used her, but were they any worse than Ogham who took away her innocence and ruined her life? No-one believed in her nobility and everyone she met treated her as a slave. Would it always be so, for the rest of her life?

As the dawn broke she fell into a fitful sleep full of strange dreams.

CHAPTER EIGHT

On the second day of Zacora's slavery in Meleagan castle she was taken to the room in which Megan entertained her clients. Harold appeared and Zacora smiled at him; that soft inviting smile which melted a man's heart and stiffened his male sword.

She was dressed in a gossamer gown which swirled around her luscious legs as she walked. Her sun-streaked hair was brushed to a glittering sheen and around her waist was a low slung belt of finely plaited silver cord. Attached to the cord was a flask, also made of silver. It was thin and light, but polished to blinding brilliance.

Harold escorted Zacora and Megan to the whoring chamber and the girl thrilled at the touch of his strong hand on her silk clad elbow. She could feel his strength, his depth of purpose. If only she could please him and him alone. Somehow she must arrange that. She sighed softly as they walked.

What thrills lay in store for him tonight, Harold wondered. He would delight in watching Megan with the customers and this new slave. He smiled down at Zacora and was rewarded with a smile of an angel.

The chamber into which they entered was dimly lit, the walls hung with red plush, giving the room a cosy glow, but Zacora shuddered.

For the first time since her capture she was free from chains, and she stretched her arms high, pressing her free breasts against the translucent gossamer of her gown. Harold watched her, very aware of the thrill he got from the delicious sight of her. She was so perfect in every way. He gazed at her willowy beauty so visible in the diaphanous gown.

She circled the chamber, examining every detail of the strange room. Harold watched her buttocks and the grace of her hips, emphasised by the silver cord hanging from the arches of her pelvis.

Zacora held up the goblet hanging from the cord, looking at it curiously, turning it in her long-fingered hands. A tiny frown line of curiosity creased the smooth skin of her forehead.

"You are wondering about the purpose of that device?" asked Harold, smiling at her.

She nodded, returning his smile.

He led her to a luxurious sofa, holding up the silver cup and admiring the fine craftsmanship which went into the making. "Megan wants you to excite her customers to the extent that they join in a contest."

Megan sniggered, rubbing her plump sex lips through the black silk of her dress.

Zacora was still at a loss and she looked at Harold to enlighten her.

"The customers stand in a line..."

"Customers?" she interrupted.

Harold sighed. "Megan likes to play at being a harlot." The whole charade was irritating for him when he wanted, so much, to take Zacora for himself, but until he he had news from the palace the time was not right.

"The customers stand in a line at the ready," he explained. "Stiff and rigid!" Harold smiled at her again, taking out his own equipment from his richly embroidered gown.

"Oh," sighed Zacora. "Must I pleasure them with hands and mouth?"

"You do neither!" said Megan curtly. "It is for me to cosset my customers with my mouth or stroke them with hands dressed in leather, silk, fur or velvet. Whatever pleases them. You will be chained to the wall as an added bonus to my pleasuring."

Harold nodded. "The goblet is to collect the spume of their lust."

Zacora looked at both her captors. "But it is a drinking goblet."

"And you shall drink, my dear," said Harold, lying back on the sofa.

Zacora's sapphire eyes, lashes lowered, focused on the beauty of his penis, rearing mightily from his lower belly. Since Ogham stole her virginity her experience of male organs had increased enormously, but Harold's was beautiful. It wasn't simply its size, but the throbbing power which it exuded. The sight of it made the melting feeling spread from her belly to her whole body.

The huge oak doors of the chamber swung open and three men swaggered in. "Ah, Megan's first gentlemen callers of the evening," said Harold, raising to greet them. "Please feel free to be casual," he invited, letting his own gown swing open again. He turned to Megan. "And begin the girl's preparation."

Megan strutted across to the visitors, her plump body lush in its near nakedness. The tight suspender belt cut into the flesh of her waist as the attachments to her black stockings framed the darkness of her bush. She posed her heavy breasts and fingered her huge nipples to hard erection. Harold gave her pillowed buttocks a playful pat and she grinned at him coquettishly as she passed. The three arriving customers were given the full treatment!

Zacora bowed her head as Megan had instructed her and unfolded her willowy body to stand upright. The diaphanous gown was held closed by only three fastenings at the front so it was a simple matter to slip it from her shoulders, leaving her clad only in the belt and goblet. This silver item lay a little below her silver fronded mound. In the subdued lighting the flesh and the metal seemed to blend into one glorious whole. The new arrivals gasped in sheer delight and hurried to make themselves comfortable and casual as Harold suggested.

Megan led her new sex slave to a shallow alcove lined with red plush. There were silver cuffs at four places in the alcove and at the centre of those four points there was a solid silver ring, large enough to be snapped around a small waist.

"Will you hold her ankles?" Megan asked two of the newcomers.

They were only too eager. "We shall be placing her upside down, you see," Megan went on to explain. "Legs nice and wide to fit in the upper cuffs."

The silver cuffs were snapped shut. Zacora was trapped with her long legs splayed wide open. The plush tickled the fine skin of her back. It was not an unpleasant sensation, but she could feel the blood rushing to her head and she could only see vague shadows of the men through her silver curtain of hair.

"Hm," murmured Megan, "yes, a delightful sight." The dew of mild excitement was gathering on the silver fronds of Zacora's sex. Between swelling flushed leaves could be seen the tender bud jutting from the fine silk of the hood.

"Mistress," groaned Zacora, "my ankles ... my legs."

"Hush, my dear," warned Megan, "you must show these nice gentlemen how you enjoy our little games."

The hanging girl arched her supple body, using her free hands to part the curtain of hair, to look up at the mistress and her men. "I find them stimulating, mistress," said Zacora, "but the ache..."

"Very well," said Megan, quickly clasping the tight waist band to give more support. "The girls today," she grumbled, "no stamina."

The two men nodded vaguely in agreement, but their eyes were focused firmly on the moist silkiness of Zacora's open sex.

The sapphire blue eyes, taking in the scene of the softly lit room in a reversed position, saw Harold lie back contentedly to stroke his rigid shaft. Zacora felt proud of the pleasure she was so obviously giving him. She saw his eyes rest on the tight belt which clinched her waist. Breathing deeply, she felt her firm breasts peak with flushed and hardened nipples. She saw him smile as he focused on the depth of the valley between her creamy hillocks. Their firmness meant that the valley was unmarred.

She watched his hand slide over the moist globe of his penis. He looked down upon it, his eyes bright with self satisfaction. Zacora's body ached to feel it plunged inside her, her flesh enclosing it eagerly to pleasure him.

Megan, aided by the men, was clasping Zacora's slender waist in such a way, with elbows bent close to the plush wall, as to increase the pouting of her breasts. She gloried in her display. Her eyes turned to Harold, wanting him to admire the way she was displayed, so open for him. Although there were others in the room, they did not matter to her.

She saw his eyes rest on the goblet, hung on the fine silver cord. Zacora could feel it resting between her breasts and knew that it enhanced the depth of the valley. It seemed to lie there, waiting to be filled.

The great oak doors opened again from time to time, allowing in other eager customers. Zacora saw their eyes drawn to the sight of her suspended in the alcove. She felt beads of her sex sap ooze from the swelling leaves of her pouch. Her long training in the pleasure of men ran deep.

"Please," she heard Harold invite, "feel free to release your cocks." His voice was husky and lazy.

She heard sighs of relief and realised what effect the sight of her in the tortuous position must have had on their male swords. Suddenly, they were all released, gleaming ad rigid.

"Are we allowed to...?" asked one. She felt him stroke her splayed legs and her fully revealed sex pouch. She felt her flesh flutter in excitement. "May I touch further? Investigate?"

"If you must, Benedict." Zacora could hear the testiness in Megan's voice. There was envy in the attention being drawn away from herself.

She recognised the man. He had been close to the podium at the auction. His eyes had never left her through that long morning.

Her puffy sex lips quivered as he touched them, massaging their firmness and stroking the firm silver down which fringed them. Zacora caressed the finger which sank into the smooth moistness of her vessel. She heard him sigh, sliding the finger in and out of the clutching flesh.

"She is well-trained," Benedict murmured. "Is this your training, Megan?"

"No," interrupted Harold. "She is a Lokaran woman. They are brought up to give nothing but pleasure to their men. They are obedient and very passive." He looked scathingly at Megan. "Quite unlike our own women here in Vakir. Disobedient, wilful hussies, most of them."

Megan sniffed haughtily.

Zacora felt her sex lips parted and she posed the erect bud of her clitoris, emphasising Harold's praises. She knew that it was flushed and eager. Benedict groaned as he felt the slight movement of the bud, urgent and wanting. His touch made more of her sex sap ooze from hidden crevices, warm and milky.

The other men gathered round, watching Benedict's actions. The close investigation, after her experiences of the past few days, stimulated her as the Master in Lokara had told her it would. The more stimulation she received, after her years of training, the more she would please her eventual husband. She could feel the strong pulse in her sex bud as it swelled and became inflamed. The tight constriction around her waist, pinching the firm flesh and making her nether regions swell, caused her sex purse to pose itself, to press outwards, towards the eager man.

Zacora felt proud as she watched the men blatantly stroking their hard stems, glossing the oozing fluid around the globes and pressing the single eyes.

Megan broke the spell. "Who will be first?" she said with false gaiety. She thrust her plump dark bush at the nearest man.

Zacora saw his wistful look in her direction as he motioned that Megan should lie on the nearest sofa. It was especially designed to thrust up her pubis and open her solid thighs.

"Oh, beautiful!" sighed Megan as he thrust savagely into her. "So good, so filling." The pumping was fast and Zacora saw him close his dark eyes.

"When ... your time ... is close," panted Megan, "I want you to pull out ... and ... fill ...the goblet." She pointed to the silver cup nestling between Zacora's lovely breasts.

The man grunted his agreement, taking a quick glance at Benedict who was gently thumbing the inflamed erection of Zacora's clitoris. It seemed to her that the sight was the trigger. With an animal growl he took his penis from Megan's cushiony width and staggered the two steps to Zacora's tethered frame. Benedict, with a dreamy smile, held the goblet to receive the pearly splashes from his friend.

The issue was copious and the man was proud of the warm amount. Megan stepped from the sofa to peer into the silver cup.

"Not bad," she judged, "but you must all take your turn before the contest is done." She made a note on a parchment with a quill placed on the table for the purpose.

Zacora felt her head being lifted. "Take a sip, my dear," she said, "and test for quality."

Zacora licked her lips.

"How she longs to taste your spume," remarked Harold. "What a wonderful girl she is to be sure!" Zacora watched him caress his length and thickness, feeling proud of the compliment.

The liquid in the goblet was still warm from the man's body. It was thick and creamy and slithered easily down her willing throat. She looked to Harold, wanting his praise, and was rewarded with a smile.

He was watching avidly, stroking back the richly embroidered silk of his robe to bare his handsome body. Zacora could only imagine the wonderful drawing sensation she felt in his groin. His penis remained a monument to his pleasure, rising, thrust from the lushness of his groin. It was a proud thickness and a full nine inches in length.

Licking her lips, she watched him stroke the silky smoothness of the circumcised tip, neatly cut to make him sensitive to every stimulation. It was moist now, pearly with male dew.

A smile softened the hard features and Zacora returned his smile. How different was his strength from the Prince who had fought so hard to purchase her. He smiled again, a secretive smile, and if Zacora had known his thoughts her ecstasy would have been uncontainable. Harold's aim was to dethrone the poor weak soul who desperately needed an heir to retain the respect of his people. Harold would produce his own heir with this beauty and combine the Meleagan lands with the neighbouring principality.

The splendour of his penis reared up and made Zacora's belly melt with need. His eyes never left the beauty of the tortured girl. Her position, to her, was no torture. She was giving pleasure to the man she desired.

She gave no hint of pain or fear. There was no pleading to be set free. Held fast by the manacles, her limbs shaping a cross, her passive beauty was unmarred apart from thin red welts across the creamy naked breasts. Those were placed there by Megan because the girl, at one stage, had gagged upon a goblet of seed. Zacora held the marks as trophies rather than a badge of punishment. Not a murmur had escaped her lips as the lash snaked out.

All Megan's callers had filled the goblet. The girl's wrists and ankles were reddened with the chafing of the manacles. Her slim belly bulged slightly with long confinement in the tight silver waist band. Zacora's mouth, those lovely wide and parted lips, shimmered with a dried silvery coating. Spilt semen formed a coating, beaded in places, and the girl's pink tongue licked at it, tasting the sharp saltiness which also lingered in the moistness of her mouth.

"One more, my dear," said Harold, rising slowly to his feet. "Take my robe, Aunt Megan."

Dutifully, her moist darkly fronded sex bush shining in the soft candlelight as she approached him, Megan took the robe. She felt out of sorts; very much out of sorts. She didn't like the slave commanding such adoring attention. Harold usually so cool and in control couldn't wait to take his turn.

Sniffing crossly, Megan threw the precious robe over a chair. She was supposed to be the hostess, the sexiest lover, the symbol of femininity. That wretched girl didn't have the wit to realise how suspenders framing a bushy thatch made men wish to part those curls to enter and fountain into the body behind it. She didn't realise how men loved to grip firm plump buttocks to open them; how they to use handles at the hips to lever themselves up and down at every thrust.

Megan watched through angry slitted eyes as Harold approached the hung girl. His body, although older than that of her other visitors, was splendid. Firm, with muscles sharply defined one from the other, his skin lightly oiled so that it shone at each perfectly honed ridge. It was truly magnificent, she had to admit. The waist had no hint of thickness. His buttocks were as trim as they had been twenty years before. The balls were smooth, trimmed so that they were like silk to the touch. They were taut, drawn up with supreme pleasure, and his spearhead was held by his own hands, like the weapon it was.

It, too, was oiled. It shone sleekly and this enhanced its magnificent size. Megan watched as he smeared another generous coating of oil on the whole length of it. That, Megan knew, meant only one thing. His weapon was destined, not to join the contest, to fill the goblet, but to enter a much tighter orifice.

"Open the lining of the alcove, Megan," he commanded.

She grumbled to herself. "Do this, do that," she hissed as she did Harold's bidding. "Anyone would think I was the slave, not her."

The curtain was opened and the satiated men watched with interest and curiosity to see what would happen next. Harold slid behind the screen to which the girl was firmly imprisoned. There was a square opening at the height of the tops of creamy thighs and pubis. The men pressed forward eagerly. Behind the girl they could see Harold's oiled penis, like a sexual talisman enraging reluctant male weapons, making them larger, more potent, more vigorous.

He held it, thrusting it against the cleft of the girl's buttocks, demonstrating its beauty. The other men groaned in unison as Zacora seemed to tense in her chains. This was not from horror or fear, but to attempt to position the deep, tight cleavage more readily for Harold's ease. Her body arched forward, just slightly, with the pressure from behind, rising because her limbs and waist were fixed.

The men craned their necks as Harold drooled yet more oil into the deep pit of her rear entrance, slicking it around with his long fingers. At last he was satisfied. He opened the pale cheeks with thumbs dug deeply into the flesh. The pit he sought was there, glimmering now with its coating of silky oil. At this angle, the positioning of his globe was all important.

It was tight, and she moaned in ecstasy.

Her ankles were inflamed from prolonged clasping in the tight manacles. The skin was chafed, but not broken. Her wrists, too, were sore from the beaten metal cuffs. The rigid belt did not allow any movement, but was tight, cutting into her fine pale skin. It caused her belly to swell a little and the taut skin over her rib cage was also swollen by the long imprisonment.

The moist skin lining her mouth felt dry from the copious salty fluids which she was forced to drink from the goblet. At first she thought she would gag, but after a while the taste was not unpleasant. It made her sex pouch become moist at the sensual thought of her humiliation.

There was another pleasure. Megan's callers admired her sex, displayed as it was at their eye level. It was open fully; the lips parted and moist, completely at their disposal. She found it both degrading and exciting. The feeling was similar to that which she felt in the market place. She was on display and she felt that this was right; exciting and stimulating.

Harold whispered to her again and she felt her tight passage gently stretched. The oily lubrication which he had generously lathered into her, made her lean back upon him as he requested.

At last he slid into her. She held him to the hilt and he groaned ecstatically. As he promised, he slid his lubricated fingers to the front, to the splayed mound with the soft down of silver fronding. His long fingers massaged the swollen pliancy of her outer lips, spreading them further.

For the moment he was satisfied to let his slickly lubricated penis lie in the tight, dark warmth. And for the moment he was satisfied to simply spread her love lips as far open as he could, feeling their moist velvety softness. The two were fitted together by a willing socket.

Soon his fingers slipped further, entering the depth of her female entrance, slimy with her pearly dew. Two fingers, the deft forefingers of each hand, opened the neglected entrance and he felt her mound bear upon his palms, urging him to open her more. Meanwhile, his thumbs slithered gently from base to tip of her clitoris.

This done, his shaft slid very slowly out of her until she thought that he had withdrawn altogether, but he had not. At the last moment he plunged back into her darkness, making her grunt with the force of the penetration. Several times more he took this action. It was as if he was confirming who was master, but there was no doubt in Zacora's mind and she soared to a delicious orgasm.

Harold roared his own pleasure, flushing her rear passage with spume after spume of his rich semen. For many moments after orgasm, they stood locked, the hot wetness spilling out along the small of Zacora's back. She could feel her sex flesh pulsing on his hands, still glued to the heat of that silky skin.

Megan, angry at her second place in the evening's entertainment, was ushering her callers from her chamber. "Are you going to stay attached to her forever?" she snapped over her shoulder to Harold.

"Yes," he whispered hoarsely, "that is what I should like when the time is right."

"She's a slave girl," Megan reminded him. "A sex slave, bought only for sexual pleasure."

Harold stroked the satiny buttocks which he so recently treasured with his sex weapon. "But of noble birth," he added.

"So she may say," grunted Megan disbelievingly. "What proof is there?"

"Her finely bred looks," he said, stepping down from the dais and slipping into his robe.

"Nothing to go by," sneered Megan. "Do you want her taken down?"

Harold nodded. "And let her sleep on this sofa tonight. No chaining. Her ankles and wrists have taken enough punishment."

"Not chained? Do you think that's wise?"

CHAPTER NINE

"Are you sure she won't run?"

Megan frowned at Zacora, twisting her own dark dishevelled hair around nervous fingers.

"I'd feel much happier if she was chained to the bed." She paused. "Or the wall. Anything solid." She reached out to stroke Zacora's arm and narrowed her eyes angrily as she felt the girl flinch. "Are you quite, quite sure?"

"Quite sure," answered Harold. He cossetted the girl's breasts, tracing their warm outline, their heaviness, with knowing forefingers. He felt her flesh tremble delightedly. "You won't run, my dear. Not from me?"

A barely perceptible shudder went through the lovely girl's frame. She remained still, silent with head bowed in gentle submission. At that very moment she had only one wish: that Harold would take her in his strong arms and hold her, possess her for ever.

But Megan, naked apart from her red garter belt, was quite adamant in her belief. "She should be chained, like any other sex slave." Her breasts jiggled with rage and she shook a pair of wrist manacles at him. "What's wrong with you, Nephew? Are you going soft in the head?" A light shone in Megan's dark eyes. "Are you in love?" she shrieked at last.

Hiding her expression beneath the shimmering thickness of hair, Zacora gasped. She clasped her hands more tightly at the moist swelling of her sex pouch. Her nubbin jerked tightly at Megan's words, moving slickly in its dripping nest. Could it be that Harold had such regard for her? She wanted to be sure. Ogham had betrayed her so.

"I do not wish her to be fettered," said Harold sternly. "I wish her to be washed and pampered as a princess."

He smiled into the liquid depths of the sapphire pools and received a tremulous soft curve of the pouting lips in return.

Zacora felt her full breasts become tender under the touch of his exploring fingers; felt her nipples tauten urgently at his touch. A fresh flow of her sex sap added to the pearly pools which already nestled between her folds. A warm heaviness settled at the pit of her belly, making her whole body lethargic and ready for him. She felt herself swaying towards him.

"Yes, a princess," Harold went on. "For she looks and acts like a princess."

The words made Zacora soar with renewed happiness. Did this truly mean that he had regard for her? She felt him stroking the pouting cushions of her buttocks, adoring the smooth curves and spreading them wide to return to the depths of the cleft between them. She felt him probe the moistness of her rear pit, enjoying the slipperiness of his remaining issue.

Megan snorted with disbelief. There was a clatter as she threw down the manacles in disgust. "Well, I'm keeping my eye on her," she said through gritted teeth. "I don't intend to let her out of my sight."

"That goes for me," added Gareth, her miserable son. His shaft was erect as he watched Harold intimately caress the sex slave.

Surreptitiously, Zacora watched Gareth's urgent actions. She knew that it was a compliment to herself. His cockstem was bloated, the veins bulging in a tight trail along its length. The end bulb was shiny, purple and slick with a drool of issue. The lad was looking at her hungrily as he stroked the long thickness and cupped the turgid heaviness of his balls.

Harold looked at him with narrowed eyes. "We shall all take it in turn to watch over her," he said softly. "She is, after all, such a precious creature."

Restraint, Zacora pleaded with herself. Restraint. She wanted to throw herself into his strength. She felt her skin flutter as she allowed his hands the luxury of touching the slender, but voluptuous, richness of golden flesh. His fingers traced the flare of the tiny waist to the ripe shelves of the hips which swept upwards to the proud mounds of the breasts. She felt him shudder as he handled each valley and hillock of delicious flesh.

Head still bowed with sweet submission, Zacora parted her naked thighs and bore her mound down into Harold's cupped hands. He sighed in delighted gratitude. She stroked the moistness of her sex pouch over his offered hands and lifted her dainty fingers to the back of her golden mane. In this attitude of complete compliance she gave herself to him.

A flush of heat swelled the petals of her sex. Her nubbin jutted, thick and long, its tip grazing his delighted fingers. Love sap oozed over swollen female folds, pervading him in the rich aroma of wanton-ness. A barely audible mew of ecstasy heralded her orgasm, but she held back, grinding her supple pelvis in an attempt to caress her lord's shaft inviting it into her heated pouch.

"I still say that she should be shackled," hissed Megan.

Zacora closed her eyes unhappily. The rasping voice had destroyed the sensual reverie of the moment. Her body ached with the loss of climax; the grinding ache felt in her loins when need is not satisfied.

"And I say she should not," said Harold firmly.

A servant was called to lead Zacora to be sponged down. The golden haired beauty stood, head meekly bowed, awaiting whatever her owners now wished. The servant, a plain girl modestly dressed in home spun garments, eyed her charge with some distaste. Zacora ignored her stares, thinking only of Harold and the excitement which he elicited in her. It was a delight to feel the sticky heat of his issue trailing over her buttocks, her puffy sex lips, and the fine inner skin of her thighs.

"Take her to be refreshed," he ordered.

Zacora lifted her golden head as she was led from the games room. She deliberately added a more provocative sway to her walk, swinging the pouting buttocks which she knew were liberally slicked with Harold's silvery spume. She enjoyed the moistness he had conjured in her sex folds. With a little effort she could massage her nubbin with that copious lubrication. She was beginning to feel that she she had been born to please, yes, but not just men, all men, any man at all: no, she had been born to please Harold, and that is what she would do!

The sapphire eyes smiled secretively as she glided along the stone passage. She could imagine Harold sinking onto his sofa, luxuriating in sensuous dreams of their coupling interrupted by Megan. She knew that she had to find some way of separating him from the influence of this unpleasant and domineering Aunt of his and her obnoxious son. Somehow she must find a way of having Harold to herself.

She let her mind drift to his wonderfully mature body. The broad shoulders tapered to a waist which was firm and not too narrow. His stomach was flat and hard, ridged with bands of muscle. A line of dark curls led from his navel to a crisp triangle. Spearing, always spearing, was his magnificent sex sword. It was dark and smooth, summited by a bursting globe. Below were his male sacs, taut and bursting with life. He kept them smooth of hair as he did the cleft of his firm buttocks.

Zacora knew of his very sensitive place at the rear of the sacs. She would have touched it to enhance his orgasm to yet more glorious heights had Megan not interrupted their play. Her Master in the school room in Lokara taught his girls of the ecstasy to be obtained by a man when this place, hidden behind the heaviness of the sperm sacs and in front of the rear mouth, was pressed gently.

Was the combination of her beauty and her expertise enough to ensure a permanent place at Harold's side?

The dowdy little servant pushed Zacora through a low door into a dark cavernous room. Tallow sconces guttered in the walls. A perfume hung in the air, sweet and dreamy, making her feel sleepy and heavy limbed. The aroma was carried by wisps of smoke puffed from channels bored deep into the old stone walls. The swirls caressed her body like insubstantial fingers, pampering each tender place until she thought she would swoon with delight.

"Up on the bench," the servant grated. The woman's sharp fingers dug cruelly into Zacora's buttocks parting the twin hillocks. She gave a cluck of disgust - or was it envy? - as she slicked the copious juices up and down the deep cleft. "Face down," she added giving the girl a vicious push to the high stone platform.

The pleasant dreaminess was replaced by apprehension as Zacora struggled to obey the servant's bidding. Her hands touched metal manacles sunk into the cold stone and the woman in charge of her gave an unpleasant chuckle as she imprisoned slim wrists in the unyielding metal. Zacora felt her long legs being pulled roughly wide apart and her ankles fettered tightly.

"What are you going to do?" she asked plaintively.

"I have my orders," said the woman, giving nothing away.

Zacora's mind whirled with unhappiness. Surely Harold would not, after his recent tenderness, cause her any hurt. So what was this woman doing to her?

Her arms and legs were held at full stretch by the fetters. The warmth of her breasts and belly was chilled by the cold stone. The heavy perfumes pervading the room were no longer pleasant. A vice seemed to squeeze her temples, crushing her mind, numbing it until she could barely think.

A torrent of icy cold water was thrown viciously on to her body, making her gasp with shock. It did not end there. It was followed by another and another. At last the torrents ended, but freezing rivulets trickled down the hollow of her spine, seeped around the pressed mounds of her breasts and soaked the hot valley of her bottom. The long golden tresses were saturated, lying in wet ropes around her head.

Zacora began to shiver miserably.

"You girls have it too easy," rasped the woman.

"Why are you being so cruel?" asked Zacora through chattering teeth. "I've done nothing to you."

"Orders," said the woman sharply. "You've got to be cleaned inside and out."

Zacora tried to turn her head, but she was too stiff and cold and her fetters held her too tightly.

The woman went about her tasks silently, refusing to say any more. Zacora felt pressure between her splayed legs. Front and rear openings were pressed open by the bony fingers. She felt the smoothness of oil being slathered liberally at the openings and she wriggled her nether regions in anticipation of pleasurable invasions.

The servant cackled evilly and Zacora felt her vagina being plundered by a wide tube. She felt chill air whisper into the heat of her sex flesh. It wasn't an unpleasant sensation. It was strange. A narrower tube entered her rear mouth so that she was completely open and vulnerable at both entrances.

"The inner cleansing is about to begin," said the servant gleefully. "The opening tubes will be removed after the flushing and you must retain the cleansing fluid within your body until I tell you that you may release it. Do you understand?"

The servant delved between the tubes, seeking the pouting heat of Zacora's clitoris. To her shame the girl found herself urging towards the questing boney fingers. The opening up of her body was exciting her, making her want stimulation even from this cruel woman.

She nodded, acquiescing to the woman's order, feeling the chill of water trickling from her soaked hair.

A flood of warmth entered her body through the tubes, gushing and foaming over her sensitive inner skin. The tubes were swiftly withdrawn and Zacora contracted her well trained nether muscles to retain the perfumed fluids. She felt them gurgling around her intimate passages, swilling away all traces of her own and Harold's fluids. The urge to bear down was intolerable and she felt, at any moment, that she must release the contents of her vagina and her bowels. Tears joined the water already lying on her peachy cheeks, for the sensation was too great to resist.

"Hold it!" rasped the servant, clutching the flesh of Zacora's sex pouch. "It must be held until I give you permission."

In her shame the girl felt her nubbin swelling, butting at the woman's clutching hands. The sensation of the swirling fluids within the intimate passages were both painful and stimulating.

"Oh no!" groaned Zacora, feeling the growing heat in her nubbin. Her captive body strained to be free of the shackles, but the imprisonment simply added to her excitement.

"Yes, my pretty," the servant whispered in Zacora's ear. "Let your pleasure flow. Let me feel your nubbin jerk upon my fingers."

The voice had become tender, wanton, so different to the harshness of only a few short moments before. Zacora allowed her orgasm to wash over her, consume her in wave after wave of pleasurable heat.

"Yes," whispered the voice. "Oh, yes!" The servant's voice was husky now with longing. "You may let the fluids gush from your body."

With a grateful sigh Zacora relaxed her nether muscles and felt the hot foaming liquids run from her vagina and her bowel. She also felt her swollen clitoris, still jerking intensely, washed by the copious torrent of fluids.

The wrist and ankle bonds were released and the servant gently turned Zacora face up. She felt her cold, taut breasts petted by the strong hands and she looked up into features which seemed to have softened.

"My name is Hera," the servant said. "Would that I could have the release of orgasm." The woman sighed sadly. She stroked the damp silver fronds of Zacora's bush, parting the plump lips to search out the nubbin. She gazed at the inflamed bud, stroking back the hood, a strange expression of envy on her pinched features.

"Why not?" said Zacora, smiling up with inviting soft lips. How odd, she thought. Why couldn't Hera have orgasms?

"Once I was a sex slave like you." The woman began to fasten Zacora's wrists and her splayed ankles back into the manacles.

Zacora frowned wonderingly.

"Oh, I know I'm not beautiful now," said Hera, as if reading the questioning thoughts. "Bitterness is a destroyer of beauty." She began to dribble perfumed oil on Zacora's cold nakedness. The oil was warmed and caused a pleasurable shudder to ripple her taut flesh. Firm hands began to trace soothing circles around the mounds of her breasts. She closed her eyes, luxuriating in the lethargy of the massage.

"I wasn't like you," said Hera. "I was a virgin when I was sold into slavery at the auction. I wasn't beautiful, just a little bit pretty and Mistress Megan gave me to one of her customers. He was rough. He raped me and it hurt."

Zacora's mind drifted back to Ogham. Her penetration, although a little painful, had been pleasurable. Her orgasms had been many and beautifully intense, but then all her training had prepared her to enjoy coupling with a man. Poor Hera, it seemed, had no such preparation.

"So I ran away," said Hera. The memory was obviously very painful to her, but she continued to massage the tiny swell of Zacora's belly. Her strong fingers strayed down to the proud plumpness of the girl's mound, petting it and stroking the fine silver curls.

Her touch was so firm, but so sensual, that Zacora found herself urging up for more stimulation. "But they caught you?" she asked breathily, wishing her hands were free to splay her outer lips, baring her moist opening and her jerking nubbin.

Hera's own hands spread the needful parts and Zacora felt the softness of the woman's breath on her oozing flesh. A hot tongue lapped at the pouting tip of the girl's clitoris.

"My punishment was the final humiliation." Hera's voice was muffled, bitter now. Her tongue lapped expertly along the whole length of Zacora's yearning sex flesh. It darted into the dark wetness and out again to caress the jerking pip. The lapping became more urgent, more rhythmic.

"They circumcised me!"

Hera stood up, her thin face slick with sex sap, shining in the guttering light of the sconces. She looked down at Zacora's fettered body, watching the silver pad of her mound throb with orgasm. "Right here on this bench. They disfigured me here. And they ripped my pleasure bud from me."

At that moment profound climax convulsions hit Zacora's slender body, again and again. The sensations were so strong that they over-rode the horror which she felt in Hera's torture. The woman was calmly brushing the silky golden curls which streamed over the stone bench. She could never have such a climax.

There was a moment of heavy silence before Zacora spoke. "How dreadful! Will they do that to me?" She heard the tremor in her own voice.

"I do not know. You please Harold the Pretender but..."

"But what?" The sapphire eyes were wide with fear as they looked up at Hera.

"There is Megan also. Be warned. Megan is cruel and influential. Do not displease her."

The words rang in Zacora's ears as Hera returned her, bathed and scented, to the Master's presence.

To the master's presence! What bliss that was!

Zacora's hair fell in a silken sheen to the curve of her buttocks. Submissively, she placed her hands on her head, but kept her eyes lowered. Hera had fluffed the silver-fronded mound and she thrust it forward in a delicate pout, offering it prettily to Harold.

She heard him give a sigh of delight as he gestured that Hera should bring her to him on the sofa. He reached up to stroke the lush sex curls, feeling the fine coating of oil which the servant had given them as a final touch. His soft fingers were firm, but sensuous as he slipped them between the slightly parted thighs.

"Did Hera tend you well, my dear?" he asked. She felt him touch the pad of his forefinger on the tip of her nubbin.

Nodding, Zacora eased her thighs further apart, offering the whole of her sex purse to him. She tried to remain passive as he slipped a finger into her fully cleansed depths, but her lips parted in a soft oval.

"You want me to spear you, my dear?" The finger slithered in and out of her silky depths, investigating and exploring every crease and pocket.

Zacora nodded eagerly, thrusting the open, shining pouch on his questing hand. Her slender pampered body was arched; her pouting breasts full and offered gladly. Her stance, with hands clasped behind her head, made her a voluntary prisoner. Her helplessness increased her desire for his body.

Looking down, her eyes became riveted on the splendour of his male sword, rigid and dark, ready for her. It preened for her, it seemed; magnificent in its vigour.

"Cloak me with your randy flesh, my dear," he said huskily. "We shall join, you and I. My issue will flood you." His handsome ageless face creased in a smile which was almost loving, but Zacora shuddered. Hera's tale hung heavy in her memory.

"I shall be ruler of this and neighbouring lands," he told her, "and you shall be my consort."

Again she shuddered as she prepared gracefully to straddle the magnificent shaft. She kept her eyes fixed on the turgid darkness of the weapon, positioning herself over the fully stretched globe, pearly with its ooze of semen. Hands on her head, balanced on widely splayed legs, she allowed the slick globe to rest at her offered opening.

She tried not to think of Hera's terrible tale. She was sure that it was not Harold who had ordered the servant's body to be disfigured, her pleasure cut off. It must have been Megan. She was the cruel one, Harold too lenient towards his Aunt in matters of punishment.

In spite of the threat of torture on the stone slab, the loss of sexual pleasure, she knew she had to escape. If Harold truly loved her, he would not punish her when he recaptured her, but love her all the more. Her flight would make him realise how deeply she was troubled by his relationship with his evil Aunt. There was no other way to convince him of this.

She pampered his globe with her mobile labia, allowing them to flutter around his male flesh. They petted the thick stem, guiding it into her depths. Zacora heard him sigh with pleasure as he held the beautifully formed arches of her hips, to grind her down upon him.

It would be a test, she decided, clutching his thickness with strong caresses. If she escaped it would be a test that his promises of wealth and kingdoms were true. She suppressed her own sighs of longing and gave herself up to pleasuring him.

Later, when the candles had burned to waxy pools and the night was velvety black, she slid from Harold's sleeping arms. She listened. The sounds were all of deep slumber. Megan and Gareth snored softly, creating a chorus of night croaks while Harold's breathing was slow and even.

For long minutes Zacora listened to the sounds, wondering if her decision was wise. At last she decided.

Barefooted, she padded across the room to the massive doors, hoping that they would open easily. They did and she gave a silent sigh of relief.

Peeping out she saw that the long corridor was empty, peopled only with shadows thrown by the guttering sconces. The whole castle seemed silent and sleeping.

With pounding heart, Zacora sped lithely along the cold stone flags. Her golden hair, freshly washed, streamed behind her. Her full breasts were firm though heavy and gave no hindrance to her progress.

At the open portcullis she saw the shadow of a guard leaning on his pike. She halted, eyes wide with fear and ears alert for any challenge. But there was nothing. The man was asleep. She bit her soft lower lip in sympathy. His punishment would be far more severe than even Hera's. She shuddered. The sadistic ways of the Meleagans were well known, but Zacora also knew that Harold, cruel though he might be, was the disciplining father figure she sought. She felt the warmth of his copious issue drool down her thighs. And he was so sensually gifted. She allowed herself a smile at that.

It was almost dawn. Zacora shivered in her nakedness. The sapphire blue eyes blinked at the sinking bright moons of Vakir; the three silver sisters. The sky was clear and a million stars twinkled in the purpling sky and she breathed the sweet fresh air.

CHAPTER TEN

Swift footed, Zacora began to run from the looming hulk of the vast castle, and the cruelty of its Mistress.

Soon she was deep in the forest, running free. The path was stoney and fallen thorns spiked her feet and branches reached out to cut her naked skin, but she was determined to continue her quest.

So intent was she on her escape that she did not hear the rumble of wheels on the rough path. She was unaware that she was being followed until a whip snaked around her naked running figure. It caught her cruelly around the fullness of her breasts, making her cry out as her erect nipples were pinched by the flexible plaited device. The finer end slapped the swell of her belly, caressing the proudness of her mound and curling under the fullness of her pubic arch.

She was captured! Held fast, probably by one of the Meleagan household. She was lost.

An imagined dart of pain shot through her nubbin. The very place at which she experienced the greatest pleasure. That would be cut out, all over. She hung her head in shame and self pity.

"Now, my beauty," said a strange booming voice. "Where do you go to in the cold dawn?" Her captor gave a light laugh. "Dressed so, and at such a pace?"

The delicate oval of her chin was lifted by strong fingers and she found herself looking into a handsome face, but she struggled in her bindings, wriggling to free her arms. The man laughed and tugged the whip tighter, pulling her to him. His skin was warm, although naked and taut over finely honed muscles.

A gasp escaped her dry throat. She could feel his male shaft, thick and hot, rising high from his groin. She tried to look down to see the object of her curiosity. It felt strange, ridged and sharp edged.

The low laugh disturbed the night sounds of the forest and he pushed her away, posing the object of her curiosity by thrusting it out to her. She was still bound by the whip and the soft leather seemed to be tightening around her, flattening her breasts and cutting into the flesh of her belly. Her breathing was swift and shallow in her confinement.

She could not drag her gaze away from his male sword. A network of fine thongs girded the magnificent organ. He held it out to her lewdly, cupping the heavy sacs below it with one huge hand.

"Yes, this is for you, my pretty," he leered. "For you!"

Zacora mewed a wordless plea and struggled in the ever tightening coil of leather, but in spite of her fear and the loathing she felt for this stranger, there was the familiar flood of heat in her sex purse. Silky moisture seeped around her folds which swelled deliciously. Her nubbin was greatly enlarged. She could feel it probing from the plumpness of the silver fronded labia.

A flush of embarrassment suffused her creamy features. Surely, she thought, he must see the swellings. She tried to turn away, presenting the pale moons of her bottom to his gaze. She heard his laugh and felt a knowing hand between her thighs.

"No!" she cried.

"Such modesty from a woman born and raised to be pleasured," he sneered. "Do you mean it?"

Zacora knew that she did not. She wanted to be taken by this forceful rough man. Every instinct told her that she wanted to bear down on his questing fingers and open willing thighs to admit his thonged member into her opening. She frowned. He seemed to know a great deal about her.

"Who are you?"

His fingers stroked her sex leaves, parting them to expose her nubbin to the chill dawn air.

"My name is Gungdir."

He pulled her closer. His chest was broad and smooth, massively muscled and he stroked her tightly bound breasts with rhythmic movement of his body

"The atavar, the wizard who helps Odin, the god of the men of the North?" she queried fearfully.

Laughingly, he whirled her away. She spun free from the coils of the whip so fast that she thought that she would spiral to infinity. At last she fell heavily into a bed of bracken and looked up at him, her wide sapphire eyes pleading that he let her go.

His hair was long and thick, blonde like hers, but darker. The colour could be likened to spun toffee rather than spun gold. His eyes were blue, but paler. The colour was of the June sky on a cloudless day. His features were chiselled by a Norse sculptor. They were sharp as the edges of the Arctic world. On his head he wore the horns of a helmet, but they grew from his scalp, spearing from the lushness of his hair.

Zacora tried to rise from the bracken, but he waved a hand and immediately she found that she was pinioned to the ground by intricate networks of cross gartering, fastened by stakes: it happened in one magical instant.

"Why?" she muttered, lifting her head to stare up at his towering figure. "Why do you do this to me?"

The light leather thongs bit into the softness of her breasts, thrusting hardened nipples upwards offering them to the wizard. The gartering spread her legs to their fullest extent, making the silver fronded nest part fully and offering the moist flesh to his cold blue gaze.

"Quite beautiful," he murmured. "Do you feel beautiful? Yes, of course, you do. There is nothing you desire more than to be bound and humiliated, and also to be beautiful."

Zacora opened her mouth to protest, but her parted lips were plugged with a muslin bag filled with herbs. A heady perfume seeped into her nostrils, swirling into her consciousness until she entered a dream world.

A dream world in which only her sexual fulfilment mattered...

An orgasm began in her erect nipples, flowed to the tips of her tethered fingers and on down to the spread of her open legs. Only then was there the familiar molten feeling in her belly. She looked up at Gungdir, pleading that he gave her the release of his magical climax.

"You are the daughter of a Norse King," she heard. His voice boomed through the morning sounds of the forest. "Odin sent me to impregnate you with some sense."

Obediently, Zacora thrust her fully open sex pouch up to the atavar. A king! She was the daughter of a king. Was she right to want Harold after all? Should it not be the prince who should take her?

Gungdir sank between her splayed thighs and positioned his massive globe at her entrance. The silkiness of it made her gasp and she took in a great gulp of herb-tainted air. Dream images entered her mind. Ogham was tearing into her vaginal entrance, ripping open the gateway between innocence and knowledge. A pain, like a hot knife, tore through her, just as it had been when Ogham entered her. It was a pleasurable pain; one of wanting and of need.

An orgasm, swift and intense, made her pinioned body convulse. The clutching walls of her passage sucked on Gungdir's shaft, engulfing it hungrily.

"Yes, my pretty," the wizard hissed. "Ogham took you through your innocence."

Zacora flushed with embarrassment, but arched to suck harder on Gungdir's stem.

"And the slave master's wooden phallus," he went on, reminding her of her continued foolishness. "Ream upon my cockshaft as you gave that imposter your copious juices."

The more insults and humiliating memories he reined down upon her, the more she climaxed. She flooded his impaling weapon with a never ending stream of her sap. She heard again the crowd at the auction crowing their appreciation of the slave master's plundering of her body.

"Let me see," said Gungdir, slowly withdrawing his thickness from her heat, admiring the droplets of pearly dew clinging to the leather bindings on his shaft. Shining droplets mingled on its globe, her sap and his, running together on the smooth skin. "Yes," he said. "You have spumed for me quite nicely. Was it enjoyable? Did you attain orgasms such as the jailer gave you on the rack?"

Zacora stiffened at the memory of the rank filth of the cells mingling with the pungent odour of that filthy man lying atop of her. She remembered pleasuring him, felt the heaviness of his scrotum stroking her splayed buttocks, felt the hot spray of his issue drenching her helpless passage.

"Such pictures I see in your mind," whispered Gungdir, plunging into her again. The roughness of the leather bindings around his shaft grated on the soft skin of her passage, increasing the stimulation.

She opened wide her sapphire blue eyes to gaze into his ice pools, wondering if there was anything she could hide from him.

He lay on her, tweaking the pouting flesh which peeked from the network of thongs. "You seek love from Harold," he reminded her. "Just as you sought lust from the boy Ogham; excitement from the jailer and strength from the sedan bearer Wolf."

He sighed.

"You stupid girl! You clutch at a penis as though it was a magic totem to give you powers which you already possess. Methinks your training was too thorough and has made you forget your natural talents."

He bit hard on one of her erect nipples. The pain was fierce bringing tears to the sapphire eyes.

Then he began to plunge deeply into her helpless body. "My issue," he panted, "will inject some wisdom into your trustful beauty."

Zacora's mind whirled. Would she regain her noble position in the land?

He panted, pushing into her satiny folds, butting the very limits of her sex pouch. She gasped at his deep intrusion, revelling in the pleasure produced by the rough bindings about his shaft.

"You will suffer." Slick sweat dropped from his luxuriant hair at his efforts.

I already have, she thought dreamily, meeting the abrupt rhythm of his thrusts.

"Many trials will befall you." His thickness was pulsing, making the thongs grate at each inward thrust.

But I shall be a noblewoman, she thought happily, clutching his wondrously plunging flesh.

"Only then may you marry the man destined for you." He grunted loudly, pleasurably, deep and loud and she heard the copious splashes enter her.

Zacora soared. Her nubbin swelled, throbbing and burning. Her passage, swilled with his fluid and pulsed convulsively. Her orgasm was unbearably intense. It came not once, but many times until she thought she would go mad with pleasure.

At last he pulled from her and with a wave of a hand her bindings were gone, her dream over...

Her mouth was free of the herb gag...

More dreams assailed her...

Dreams that came and went; of Harold, of Gungdir. When she awoke, if she had slept, for she could never be sure, the Vakaran dawn was full. Birds sang and the spectre of Gungdir hovered above her head. She seemed to hear his voice, deep and echoing. She reached out with a creamy arm, beckoning with slim fingers, wanting him.

"You do not need me," came a whisper in her ear, so soft as to be unreal. "You have the power to rule: to be anything you wish to be."

Afraid but excited at the same time, Zacora ran on, searching for she knew not what. 'Anything you want to be,' she murmured to herself, over and over.

She was running, she knew not why.

Then at last, feet torn and bleeding, she lay panting on a mossy bank, arms outspread behind her head and long creamy legs apart, baring her silver fronded sex...

Again she slept...

Until...

"A beauty indeed, Highness." The voice was cultured and soft. "Shall we have the sergeant-at-arms take her for the harem?"

Zacora opened startled eyes which darted anxiously from one to the other of the men. She heard a gasp as they saw the deep blue of her wide orbs.

"And this, my lord ..." One of the men was stroking the softness of the silver curls between her legs. "A prize indeed! So different from the duskiness of the Vakaran women."

"Open her up fully."

Zacora looked up at this last speaker. Although he was dressed for the hunt he was clearly of noble birth. She saw his eyes glitter as they rested first on the full mounds of her breasts and then upon the silver fluff of her bush, pouting and glittering in the morning light.

"Open her up," he repeated. His voice was lowered in a husky whisper which held the firmness of command.

One of his aides knelt between her parted legs and, using both hands, pulled apart her puffy sex lips. Zacora knew that such exposure would make her nubbin swell and thrust upwards. Her sex sap oozed from the open folds.

"Delightful, my lord, is she not?" The aide turned to look at his master. "So willing to please. Surely a prize for your harem, my prince."

Zacora gave a secret smile. 'Anything you want to be.' The magical words echoed in her ears. Was this her chance to be a princess? The wizard had confused her by giving her choices.

"It would seem so," said the Prince. "Perhaps an heir will come from this meeting," he added wistfully.

The aide who held her pouch open slipped a gauntletted finger into her pulsing vagina, raising his eyebrows at the strength of the clutching. "She is but a sex slave, sire." He withdrew his finger to examine the slick. "She is unworthy of your highness. She is a trained slave."

Zacora's mind screamed at him: I am a noble, the daughter of a King. But she remained silent.

"Do you think so?" The Prince frowned. "She looks too refined, too noble." He bent to stroke her creamy skin, grazing the softness of a breast. "The Auction!" he exclaimed. "I knew she was familiar. I tried to buy her at the auction and was outbid by some merchant." He smiled triumphantly. "Bind her and have her prepared for me. His loss is my gain."

CHAPTER ELEVEN

The girl was beautiful; achingly beautiful.

"What's she called?" Callan eased his leather loin cloth to accommodate his swiftly growing erection.

"Zacora Prim," said Bernlada with a giggle. "And she is - very prim."

Callan's black eyes glinted as he stared at the girl, helpless in her induction chains. The sight of her made his muscular body tauten, ready to spring upon her. Her incredible sapphire blue eyes turned upon him, pleading for mercy. Callan shuddered as the tension in his male sword grew to the point of pain.

"How did the Prince happen upon her?" asked Callan. He placed his large hands on the glass of the viewing chamber as if he wished to break through and take the girl in his arms.

Bernlada, so long Callan's helpmate, gritted her teeth angrily. "He found her on the forest path, exhausted with her feet torn from a long run. She's escaped from somewhere, but no-one knows where."

"A neighbouring kingdom," said Callan vaguely. The girl was lovely, luscious and ripe, but slender and willowy.

A cloak of shimmering golden curls fell to her waist. The jewel-like eyes were fringed by thick dark lashes. Her nose was straight and long. Soft lips, wide and with a sheen of moisture, were parted to show white and even teeth. The high-boned cheeks were flushed in the pale face.

Callan's eyes flickered down to the naked breasts. Their upper swell rose and fell as she breathed quickly. The flushed nipples were erect and pert while the fullness beneath seemed to beckon him to cup them in his hands.

Her long slim arms were stretched tautly, one to her rear and one to the front, shackled between her widely spread thighs. The feet, so sorely used through her run through the forest, had been bandaged by a serving maid, but were, nevertheless, manacled to prevent escape.

Silvery blonde fronds escaped at each side of the wrist manacles. The curls were soft and dewy, shining in the soft lights of the induction chamber. Callan gulped. How he longed to spread that bush, open the cushiony lips to reveal the female petals and bud beneath.

His cock was at full stretch, probing open the loose loin cloth to reveal itself. He saw the girl looking at it, her eyes shining - with what? Longing? Fear? Disgust? He couldn't tell. He held his shaft loosely in both hands, displaying its length and thickness. The fingers of one hand strayed to the fullness of his sperm sac, bursting with life and power. The fingers of his other hand stroked the thickness of the end globe, spreading issue from the single eye.

He saw the girl blush, the thick lashes fluttered on the fired cheeks, but she looked at him proudly. The sapphire blue eyes focused on the display of his manhood.

Bernlada pressed against him, squeezing his body and rubbing her rounded little belly up and down his hot length. "You don't want her," she rasped in her low gravelly voice. "You and I have mated these many years past. We have weaved the magic of sex within the Prince's gates and he has never failed in the rewarding."

Callan smiled down at her small, eager face. "And we shall continue to do so," he assured her. Bernlada's body was always willing, ready and open for him. It was a vessel into which he had spilled many fountains of his seed and, by doing so in full display for the Prince, had released his Highness's inhibitions.

"Zacora Prim!" scoffed Bernlada, turning to look at the captive in the glass induction room. "Have you ever heard such a stupid name?" Her dainty little hands were cossetting Callan's beautiful rod; stroking tiny fingers up and down the silky tightness and testing the ropey veins which curled around it like a snake taking its prey.

Callan's eyes strayed back to Zacora, marvelling at her beauty. Never had he seen skin so pale and unblemished. It was so fine as to be almost translucent. Was she even of this world? Drawn to her widely splayed legs, his black orbs focused on the silver spray of her pubic curls. It was lush and prolific, but he could tell that the texture would be soft and white, unlike Bernlada's crisp blackness. If only he could enter the induction chamber, but it would be impossible until the Prince gave his permission and, even then, Callan would not be allowed to touch the gorgeous creature.

It was a torture to be so close to such lusciousness and be unable to satisfy himself, to spurt all his desires into her.

"Let me suck you to satisfaction," pleaded Bernlada. "You produce so much, so quickly, that the Prince would never know if I drank it down." The small impish woman was beginning to hate the Prince's new plaything. She knew that her own beauty, great though it was, was no match for the fettered prisoner behind the glass. She held up her heavy breasts, stroking the saucer-like nipples to swift and hard erection and brushed them coaxingly against the muscular width of Callan's chest. He smiled at her again and took her in his arms before pushing on her narrow shoulders.

"Drink me down," he agreed, but he did not look at her. His handsome black eyes were focused on the haughty beauty behind the glass. Would that it was her milky skin brushing his tall and muscular smoothness. Would that it was her hands clutching his leather thronged calves and lifting his loincloth.

Bernlada's black mane brushed his thighs as she nuzzled into position and and Callan shuddered. The brisk little beauty had served him well over the years as his helpmate, but he needed a change and the ripe peach behind the glass would suit him nicely, if only he could find some way to persuade the Prince that she was not for him.

The soft moist caress of Bernlada's tongue made its first essay on the tense sperm sac drawn up between Callan's thighs. He shuddered. She had a magic touch. Indeed, there was a time when he thought that she was the assistant of Hell, the goddess of Death, but it was her appearance, her swarthiness and her healing touch which made him think thus.

Now the sperm sac was engulfed entirely by Bernlada's full mouth. Callan squatted, urging her with rhythmic writhing of his perfect body, to take all of his maleness into her accommodating mouth. Slowly, like a python engulfing a victim, she swallowed the length and girth of his shaft, adding it to his balls in the sucking maw of her mouth.

Callan felt a feeling of triumph as he watched Zacora shift in the chains which held her bandaged feet. Was it his imagination or was she gently swaying her wrist chains back and forth through the silvery fronds of the forest between her spread thighs? Could he truly see the dew of excitement shining on the soft strands? Was her female bud probing through the blonde curls jerking for attention, and were the protective lobes swelling around the tight chains that kept her arms fast between her legs? She gave him a soft smile and he could take the strain no longer. He felt his penis jerk in the depths of Bernlada's throat and she pulled back, an angry snarl distorting her dark beauty.

"Too soon!" she hissed. She sat back on her heels, her thighs spread wide and her tiny fingers opening her nether lips to release the dark purple of her womanhood. She rubbed it impatiently, looking up at him with her green cat-like eyes.

Unable to hold back, Callan held the pulsing thickness of his weapon, allowing its spume to fountain high into the air. It glowed with power. A pearly heat produced steam which flowed around them, engulfing them like a morning mist.

Mouth open, like a hungry fledgling, the captive watched his climax, which seemed endless. It poured, as a stream in flood, over Bernlada, soaking the coal black mane of her hair, trickling over her bursting breasts and coating the swell of her belly.

"Yes," she rasped, arching up to allow his torrent to fill her pulsing vessel. Her agile fingers had brought on her own climax. It was the rule that Callan's issue should always be collected in Bernlada's urn. The Prince had decreed this rule.

The torrent slowed and Callan's eyes became less glazed, but still he stared through the glass. The captive had bewitched him. The chain, cutting into her female bloom, was shining with her juices, and the pink bud was clearly visible through the silver fronds of her patch.

Bernlada carefully folded the black leaves to conserve Callan's spume within her body. The Prince was convinced that it had magical properties and he ruled that it must be spread upon his cock every night by Bernlada herself.

The swarthy beauty rose gracefully to her feet, holding her sex purse closed with one hand. "Did you see how much he poured into me?" she rasped to the captive. "Do you think you could cause him to be so vigorous?" Her voice was harsh and cruel in her challenge. "I know you could not. With me, he cannot hold back his love juice. The very sight of me makes him spurt."

Callan said nothing, hoping that Bernlada would not notice the swiftly growing bulge beneath his loin cloth. His imagination was running havoc with his blood. There was fire in it, and it was filling the network of vessels around his cock until he thought they would burst.

A small hand slapped down on the thick spike which stood out like a sconce from the palace wall, lifting the thin soft leather of his loin cloth. "Enough of this!" rasped Bernlada. "You wretch! We'll see what the punishment mistress can do with you, because I'll not take more of your nonsense."

"Yes, Bernlada," said Callan. His voice was firm, but dreamy.

"You are mine. Even your thoughts are mine."

"Yes."

"Then why are you thinking of the captive? The Prince caught her for himself. You know how much he needs an heir."

Callan looked at the ripe beauty behind the glass and his black eyes had an expression of longing. "Why does he need my help? Or yours?"

"As a couple, we inspire him." Bernlada said proudly. "But he needs a beautiful woman to bear him a son."

"He has his pick of beautiful women, but none bear fruit." Callan imagined how it would be to plunge the long girth of his flesh sword into the moist spongy depths of the captive. She had shown that she was ripe for his taking.

Bernlada's hand took a firmer hold on her dripping sex. "I know and I also know that the Prince is afraid for his potency, but enough discussion. I must put you with the punishment mistress."

Callan saw Zacora's eyes widen with fear as Bernlada led him away. He smiled reassuringly and mouthed the message: "I'll be back!"

She looked so vulnerable in her bonds and her body looked so ready to take his that the thought of pain and bondage in the dungeons held no fear for him. He would simply fill his mind with thoughts of the captive girl.

"I don't see what's so wonderful about her," muttered Bernlada. "Am I not beautiful?"

"Of course you, are my precious little one," he soothed. He watched her neat tight bottom roll rhythmically from side to side as she walked ahead of him along the panelled passage. There was a tiny dimple in each cheek, emphasising the dark plumpness. The crevice between the buttocks was deep and Callan knew that the intimate pit which nestled in that crack was as willing and accommodating as the front orifice. Bernlada's waist was almost shocking in its severity; a hollow separating the swell of the hips from narrowness of the thorax, and yet there was nothing narrow about the breasts. These were comforting pillows of flesh, soft but firm, lifted high by their youthful tone. The tumbled black mane fell from the crown of her head to well below her shoulders, glossy and bouncing on her swarthy skin.

In repose, Bernlada had the face of a dark angel. It was gentle and soft, begging to be stroked and caressed. The brown eyes were limpid pools of warmth in which Callan had sometimes drowned in dreams.

But there was a problem. Bernlada had a fierce temper. When she was in the throes of a tantrum her eyes became as black as coals. She hissed and spat like a beast which was part cat and part snake. Her tiny hands became claws, reaching out to slash and maim. The shapely body weaved this way and that as she attempted to attack an enemy.

They reached the narrow steps that led to the dungeons of the palace of Vakir. It was cold and damp and Callan shuddered. He knew that there were subjects who spent years in the dungeon, ending their lives there. Bernlada stroked his thick, muscular arm, feeling the tanned skin.

"Goose-bumps," she giggled. "Fear or cold, Callan? Surely not fear in my courageous, virile lover."

Derision made her deep husky voice more rasping. Only the thoughts of the chained captive, so blonde, curvaceous and vulnerable, kept Callan from smashing Bernlada with a hammer-like fist. It wouldn't help the poor creature should he bring down more anger upon her.

"Cold," he said softly. "Maybe the punishment mistress would be so kind as to give me warmer clothing."

The little minx at his side sniggered. "I'll see what I can do." Her voice had a sneering grate.

There was a distant scream, pain-filled and desperate, as they trod the uneven stone passage. Pleading groans echoed through the vast chambers. The air had a musty smell tinged with the metallic odour of blood.

"Here we are," said Bernlada cheerfully. She still held her sex pouch tightly closed with one hand. "Goodness, Callan, you really drenched me today. The Prince will be pleased." She opened a heavy iron door with her free hand. "I want this man well and truly disciplined," she said to a heavily muscled figure in the corner of the big room.

Callan was perplexed. "Why do I need to be disciplined when the Prince will be pleased?" He adjusted his loin cloth at the sight of the punishment mistress and wished his weapon was less defenceless.

"You have displeased me, you handsome idiot!"

"But you said I'd drenched you," he protested. "You should be pleased."

"You've been unfaithful in thought."

The punishment mistress stepped forward. Callan gasped at the sight of her. Her beauty was undeniable, but her power and obvious strength were overwhelming, even to someone of Callan's attributes. She was over six feet in height, heavily muscled and clad only in a tight leather leotard. Her full breasts were bare, protruding from carefully cut holes. On her arms she wore many gold and enamelled slave bracelets. Her waist was cinched with a silver chain-mail belt. The honed muscles of her legs were criss-crossed with leather thongs in which were inserted daggers and whips of various kinds. The fiery red hair was twisted into a heap upon her head, and in this, too, there were many instruments of torture.

"Do you require simple bondage, madam?" she asked, looking Callan up and down. "Or was there something more elaborate?"

The look made Callan shudder. She was appraising him; seeing how much pain he could take.

"He has been a thorough nuisance since the Prince brought the new captive to the palace," said Bernlada in a spiteful tone.

"I understand, madam."

"I thought you would, Freya," said Bernlada. "You've never failed me yet." She turned to leave and then stopped in her tracks. "He says he's cold. Put him in something warm." She smiled evilly. "I think you know what I mean."

"Of course, madam." Freya lifted Callan's loincloth and cupped the sperm sac. "Leave it to me."

"Enjoy yourself," said Bernlada as she left the cavernous room. They heard her chuckle as she hurried to the Prince's chamber.

"Take off the loin cloth," ordered Freya. She stood straight and tall on high-heeled boots, legs stretched wide. Callan saw her hand stray to her waist and wasn't surprised to see the leather leotard part and reveal the smooth flesh of her flat belly as she slowly unzipped it. Down, down, down slid the zip until the fiery red bush of Freya's sex probed puffily out of the narrow slit.

With deft finger and thumb Callan released the knot in the fine leather thong which kept his loin cloth in place. Although flaccid and drooping his sex club was thick, long and magnificent. A pearly drop of dew hung heavily from the smooth, beautifully circumcised globe. Freya lifted the club and examined the slit. "Nice," she said appreciatively. "Rub it for me. I want it thick and hard. My sex muscles will drain you. It is necessary before I begin your punishment programme."

Callan raised a querying eyebrow. "The supply of my issue is not endless, mistress," he protested. "Bernlada has taken a great deal this very morning."

A deep-throated disbelieving laugh echoed through the high-vaulted room. "Are you trying to tell me," said Freya, giving him a wide-eyed smile, "that the famous Callan can only give one stream of issue in a day?"

His dark eyes stared at her stonily, suddenly hating this kingdom ruled by an impotent Prince and dominated by women. In his mind he saw the blonde captive sitting in the induction cell, waiting so passively for her fate. The thought spurred his flesh sword and it rose magnificently. It lay flat against his belly, quivering as its girth steadily increased.

"Beautiful," said Freya. Her eyes sparkled with interest and Callan saw her big hands spread the fiery curls to reveal the many-leaved pouch at the open crotch of her leotard. "A glorious manhood. See what you can do when you put your mind to it?"

An unbidden smile curved Callan's handsome lips. His mind was on the pliant Zacora who he knew he could love as he pleased. She would obey him, do his bidding. If only he could have her forever, for himself alone.

"I shall display my body to you to the utmost," said Freya coldly. "I am extremely fit and flexible, as you will see." She plumped out the thick lips more fully from the tight confines of the leotard. The red curls glinted with her moisture.

In spite of the massiveness of his erection, Callan felt no desire for the woman. Only the beautiful vision of Zacora in his mind made him able to produce any semblance of enthusiasm.

Freya slowly arched her body backwards. Her long legs were splayed widely apart on taut muscles. She clutched her ankles and her open sex pouted moistly at him.

He poised at her offered entrance, noticing the unusual nature of her. The labia were many and were frilled. They fluttered in gentle caresses around his globe, petting the tight, moist skin. Callan found himself mesmerised by the rhythmic movements of the labia. They cossetted him, drawing his sword into the deep, moist scabbard.

"Deeper," growled Freya. "Give it to me to the hilt. To the hilt, man!"

It was then that Callan realised that he had been somewhat fearful of the punishment mistress's body. He drove into her, deep and hard, leaning over her bowed body. His dark pubic curls grated against her fiery red ones and they seemed to enmesh, binding their bucking bodies together.

Freya arched up yet further, pressing him upwards. The fluttering labia, wet with her female spume, sucked at his cock. The caresses were soft at first, stimulating the whole length of his stem. The sensation made Callan feel faint with delight, he went fuzzy and his mind was less than clear. Who was he spearing?

The fluttering sensation around his embedded penis increased. It became firmer, seemed to suck him. He groaned, trying to draw back, but he was held fast. There was a delightful, and yet painful, pulling sensation in his sperm sac. It felt that the whole contents were being drawn by the fluttering leaves of Freya's sex. He groaned again, louder this time.

"Let it go," breathed Freya softly, and her voice sounded far away.

Callan's orgasm was intense. It built to a crescendo of glorious sensation and left him hovering there at a peak which seemed to go on forever. The beauty of the spasms was so gorgeous, that for the moment he cared not whether he survived the coupling, and it felt that he would not.

The flooding which he gave Freya was at least as great as Bernlada's, but the punishment mistress commanded more. "You're not trying, Callan," she rasped. "A puny effort for someone of your reputation. I have climaxed three times to your one."

Sweat glossed the magnificently honed muscles as he pounded into her. His breathing was ragged and rapid. "Give me strength!" he pleaded. His fingers dug into the tense flesh of her buttocks as he tried to gain more purchase to do her bidding.

"You have strength, you wretch," she hissed. "You are becoming lazy in your easy task with the Prince."

Callan's world seemed to have narrowed to the fiery red sex purse into which he poured his spume. The sucking, fluttering labia were gobbling his long thickness until he thought that it would be torn whole from his over-pleasured body.

"I am spent, mistress," he groaned. "I have no more for you." Still shuddering from orgasms which blended, one after the other, into an exhausting whole, he slid to the floor. His majestic shaft twitched miserably at his groin, half its normal size and thickness. Its skin was no longer taut, but wrinkled and steamy wet.

Sighing, Freya stretched upright, folding the still fluttering labia inwards, to hold Callan's spume safe in her body. "I suppose that will have to do," she said sadly.

"May I go now?" Callan wished to ensure that his beauty, Zacora, was safe. If he made careful plans they could, perhaps, escape together.

Freya looked down at him, surprise and scorn marring the beautiful face. "Go?" she queried.

On his feet now and beginning to tie his loincloth back in place, Callan felt his strength beginning to return. "Yes, go," he answered forcefully. "You have finished with me."

"I most certainly have not," Freya denied. "I have a full programme of punishments for you." She tugged at the leather thong around his waist leaving him naked once more. His sex sword was filling and was almost restored to its usual glory. She whipped it, catching the circumcised globe with her strong fingers. "And this, you wretch!" she screamed. "You told me you were spent. You are obviously not, you lying knave."

Callan squared up to her, glaring into her angry face. "You're beautiful when you're angry," he said, with an impertinent smile.

The remark took the punishment mistress by surprise, took her off guard. He watched her features soften and saw her preen the crown of red curls on her magnificent head. Her mouth softened to a moist pout and she smiled coyly.

"May I kiss you?" asked Callan, stepping towards her.

Freya nodded, her expression almost modest and maidenly. She lifted her hands and placed them behind her head, offering herself to him. The position made her lovely breasts more vulnerable, pressed out through the holes in the fine leather leotard. The nipples, a delicate peach, were hardened nubs begging to be sucked.

Fully erect again, Callan pressed against the firm flatness of her belly. He could smell the tangy odour of leather of her leotard and the strong female musk of her excitement. His strong hands grasped the offered breasts, squeezing them violently. He heard her murmur, but he was unsure whether in pain or ecstasy. Dipping his head, he took a nipple in his mouth, caressing it with tongue and lips. Freya pressed forward, forcing more of the breast flesh into his mouth. He tasted milk, sweet and warm, and he sucked contentedly, feeling his eyes droop as he became pleasantly sleepy.

He had a plan. He knew he had a plan. A plan to escape with Zacora. He was going to open Freya's zip to release a torrent of his sperm. In the ensuing mayhem, with Freya ecstatic in his issue, he would be gone.

But somehow it didn't seem important any longer...

Why did he want to escape, he asked himself, nuzzling into the warm pillow of Freya's breasts? He had everything he wanted here: nourishment, warmth, love.

The warm milk trickled down his eager throat and he became sleepier. Never in his life had he needed sleep so much. Dreams clouded his consciousness; dreams of a beautiful girl. Zacora Prim. Who was she? It didn't seem to matter any more. Nothing mattered except the comfort of the breast and the warm, delicious milk.

Finally, consciousness left him completely.

CHAPTER TWELVE

The big man, Callan, had promised he'd return, thought Zacora miserably. But he had not done so. Her willowy body was cramped by her bonds. The chain holding her wrists between her splayed legs were designed not to allow her to stand straight. Or rather she could stand straight, but if she did, her pink and tender sex flesh would be cut cruelly by the cold metal of the chain.

A twinge of pain from one of her torn feet made her wince and give a soft moan. The way from the Meleagan's castle had been paved with stones and thorns, but she had been determined to escape.

The Meleagan family were descendants from the knight who captured the Queen. Their sadistic ways were well known, but Zacora found that Harold was the man she sought: a disciplining father figure who was sensually gifted.

Zacora sighed deeply and this deep intake of breath caused the wrist chains to grate against the delicacy of her female bud. She felt it draw out excitedly from its hood and she repeated the movement, for it made her think of the tall, handsome man who had gazed at her so kindly through the glass.

But he had not returned.

She felt the chain cut into her bottom cleft and graze her rear bud. The links of the chain were large, smoothly rounded, designed, it seemed to cause pleasure as well as pain. One loop probed into her rear opening, making it throb around the cold metal. She pressed harder, allowing the loop to enter her ready rear. The sensation was pleasant, comforting, and brought back the vision of two men who desired her so clearly. Both so different. She imagined the loop of chain to be their flesh swords, probing and caressing the narrow openings, front and back.

In her imagination she could feel their hard male bodies pressing against her helpless one and their cocks probing deep into her moist warmth. Why did she also crave the servant when Harold was the one she loved? Why did she crave rough handling when Harold knew exactly how to pleasure her? All her life she had given pleasure, perhaps, and now she was greedy to take it.

Quietly, she felt the wave of climax engulf her and she whispered her pleasure. The shudders which rippled through her lovely body made the chain catch the raw bud of her naked clitoris. Again, a pleasure wave rode through her, racking the delicious flesh with indescribable sensation. She revelled in it, but she dare not reveal how great her enjoyment.

"Now, my beauty," rasped a woman's voice behind her.

The silvery blonde hair swirled around Zacora's head as she tried to spin around to see her attacker, but her bandaged feet were held fast by the ankle manacles.

Leather gloved hands slid around her naked body and grasped the firm fullness of her breasts. As much as she was able Zacora struggled in her bonds, but said nothing. In truth the softness of the leather and the delicacy of the touch was pleasant to the highly receptive girl.

There was a hoarse laugh. "No need to struggle, Miss Prim - that is your name is it not?"

Zacora's nipples glowed and hardened, but she remained silent. Her breasts swelled against the caressing fingers, pouting proudly, and she prayed that the woman, whoever she was, would not notice the unbidden reaction. She offered up a further silent prayer that the leather-clad fingers would not investigate further, would not stray to the silver cloud of pubic curls and what lay beyond. If the sensitive digits probed the wet pinkness her excitement would be revealed.

As suddenly as her breasts were grasped they were released and Zacora heard the click of high heels on the floor of the chamber. Keeping her head bowed, she saw neat black leather boots planted firmly apart in front of her. Allowing her eyes to lift a little she saw that the boots were long like the legs which they clad. A finger lifted her trembling chin, forcing her to look upwards. There was a soft gasp of surprise.

"Oh!" heard Zacora. "They told me you were beautiful, but this!" There was a pause, then the woman spoke again. "My name is Paige. I prepare the Prince's young ladies for coupling with him."

With eyes made wide with the fear of the unknown, the girl looked up at the woman. She could feel hot tears stinging the soft sapphire blue eyes and, mutely, she pleaded for mercy.

"You're like an angel," came the whispering voice. "Surely you did not issue from any human womb?"

Zacora, lips parted, looked up at the woman. Her limbs were cramped terribly, for she had been chained in this position for several hours. Apart from the serving maid who had tended her feet and the man who lusted after her she had seen no-one until now. With a slow bend of her long spine she tried to make the heavy chains rattle to convey her extreme discomfort. The cold links brushed lightly against the heat of her sex flesh and made her shudder with unbidden pleasure.

A hand stroked the glossy platinum of her hair. "You poor thing!" said the woman. "You must be aching like mad. I'll have something done about it."

Zacora heard other footsteps, lighter, as though the wearer wore soft shoes. There was no harsh clack of heels, only a whispering, padding sound.

"Look at me," ordered the woman. "You are a lovely creature. Can you talk?"

The girl looked up, fixing her limpid sapphire orbs on the woman, and shook her head, for the time being she had decided that until her thoughts were put in order she would not speak.

"You poor thing!" The woman seemed kind and caring and Zacora gave her a slight smile. Two gentle hands released the shackles between her straddled thighs. It was a relief to be able to stretch and she did so, straightening her long slim back and drawing herself up tall. She felt her heavy breasts tauten on her delicate rib cage as she eased her cruelly tortured spine. The very slight swell of her belly flattened as she arched upwards. She felt the soft pad of her mound contract and the silver fronds of her bush flutter with the movement.

"You may roll the manacles in the flesh of her pouch," said Paige to the serving maid who was releasing Zacora. "I wish to check on the state of her arousal."

Tears filled the blue eyes, for the order took her back to the school room in Lokara, in the time only days ago, although it seemed like months or years. The Master who taught the girls pleasure would check on their arousal. But life then was so innocent and her innocence, she felt, had gone forever.

The serving maid was small and plump, with a round cheerful face. Zacora looked down at her, trying to convey her unhappiness and pleading that the ravishment should not be too intimate.

"Bend your legs, dear," said Paige softly, "and let Bella squat between them."

Obediently, Zacora allowed her knees to relax, giving the serving maid more space to intrude in the sleek arch of the lovely limbs.

Keeping her sapphire blue eyes to the front, the girl did not look at either Paige or Bella. She knew that the silver fronded portals were spread, displaying the fresh moist folds and the jutting bud which nestled between them.

"Could you give your pelvis more frontal exposure, dear?" requested Paige sweetly. "I want to see all there is to see of that pretty little pouch before Bella does her tests."

Fresh tears made the wide eyes more lustrous. Patches of red appeared on the high cheek bones as Zacora did as she was ordered.

"Tears?" questioned Paige. "Why so? Bella will not hurt you."

"No, mistress," smiled Bella, looking up at the parted sex leaves with their shimmering coat of dew. "She is too pretty to be disfigured."

"You see!" Paige was triumphant. She was resplendent in a tightly-laced and boned black satin corset. The garment left her breasts and sex bush naked, jutting out and begging for attention. The breasts were firm and large, centred with dark brown buds decorated with small gold rings which pierced the erect flesh. The bush was thick and lush, the curls braided with precious stones which sparkled and danced as she moved. The long boots reached her sex and the cuffs were designed to spread the folds open. Paige's face was handsome, the dusky skin stretched over beautifully carved bone structure. The fine features spoke of mixed race, but high birth. A small crown of gold held back the lustrous mane of crinkly curls.

"Rub the chains within the folds, Bella," ordered Paige. "And let me sniff the perfume of her musk."

Zacora's head reeled at the command. She didn't care for the intimate touch of women. Men, with their penetrating organs, their rougher fingers, their fumbling investigations and their shouts of triumph as they spumed their semen, men were much more satisfying. She closed her moist eyes, trying to shut out the women and their actions.

"You must watch," hissed Paige. "It is imperative, just as it is imperative for me to watch your reactions."

Reluctantly, Zacora opened the tear-dewed lashes and looked down at the serving maid who cupped the wrist manacles in her small hands and edged the bundle of metal towards the unwillingly displayed sex. Tense with apprehension Zacora flinched away.

Paige laughed. "So it's true what they say about you," she scoffed. "You really are Miss Prim!"

Biting her full bottom lip Zacora tried to be obedient, offering the frontally presented softness of her sex to the invading metal of the manacles. The links of chain were cold against the moist heat of her and the folds of her pouch fluttered against the intrusion, grappling with them softly.

"Aaah," breathed Paige excitedly, stepping forward to watch more closely. "Not so prim, after all. See how the folds caress the chain, Bella?"

"Indeed, Mistress."

Paige stroked her nipple rings, allowing her leather-clad fingers to trace the outline of the finely beaten gold. "Perhaps, at last, we have found the female who will beget the Prince an heir." Her handsome features smiled kindly at Zacora. "Think how wonderful would be your position in the kingdom if he sired a son on you."

Once more, thought Zacora, I am to be a slave. My body is not my own. Oh, how I long to escape these lands ruled by despots and cruel knights. Only one man had grasped her heart and that was Harold; one man and the handsome slave who, perhaps, she dreamed, could be Harold's squire.

"Give me the chains, Bella," said Paige coldly. "I shall test the aroma and you..." She paused, her almond-shaped eyes, dark as the deepest pits of hell, slitted with anger. "And you must whip her."

Bella, full cotton petticoats rustling as she rose to her feet, grinned eagerly.

"But on no account must you mark her," warned Paige. "The Prince will be displeased if he receives damaged goods."

"Of course, mistress," agreed Bella. "I shall choose only the softest of whips. It will merely caress her skin, remind her that she belongs to the Prince."

"I could tell by the expression on those perfect features," said Paige huskily, stepping close to Zacora, "that you were rebelling." The manacles were held to the long dusky nose and the perfume was sniffed hungrily. A smile wreathed the dark features, analytical and knowing. "You seem to be easily stimulated," she surmised.

Zacora held her breath with relief. At least Paige had not realised that some of her stimulation came from her own thoughts of Harold, not from Bella's caresses.

"How would you care to see her whipped, mistress?" The plump little maid was beaming with eagerness, her round face flushed with barely suppressed excitement.

The captive girl watched, trembling, as Bella tucked her full petticoats into a tightly cinched belt. Horror made the sapphire eyes widen to their fullest extent as she saw how the maid's sex was treated. A solid metal block, obviously tailored to fit by a skilled iron smith, covered the folds from front to rear. It was held in place by a leather harness around the waist and top of chubby thighs.

"She is quite used to it," said Paige matter-of-factly, following Zacora's horrified gaze. "It causes her no discomfort - now." She sniffed at the delicate musk still exuding from the chains. "I expect at first it was a little uncomfortable."

Bella gave a barely perceptible nod. "You might find out what it's like, if you don't please the Prince."

The sapphire eyes darted from one to the other of the two women, querying what a female must do to prevent such treatment. Zacora felt herself tighten with fear; the moist passage closing involuntarily and the bud hiding amidst the pink folds.

Finishing with the chains, Paige discarded them and brushed her naked breasts against Zacora's. The captive felt the strangeness of the gold nipple jewellery whispering against her unadorned breasts. "Press up your pouch as high as you can," said Paige in a soft command. "Let me feel your buttock cleft pressing to the front."

Bella was hopping impatiently from foot to foot behind them. "The whipping, mistress," she reminded Paige, "the whipping!"

"You impetuous little minx!" chided Paige. "Be still until I'm ready." She gyrated her jewelled bush against Zacora's carefully posed sex pouch, making the soft silver fronds excite the sensitive pink flesh until the captive girl began to shudder with the stimulation. "Bella loves to punish," explained Paige. "She was one of the Prince's potential consorts, but like all the others, she failed to produce an heir. The block is her punishment."

If Paige had not been ready to hold her, Zacora would have collapsed with shock. As it was she felt the blood drain from her already pale features; felt her mouth become dry and her tongue cling to the roof of her mouth.

"But never fear," soothed Paige, "we shall prepare you so that you will not fail."

Had she been able to speak Zacora would have asked why the punishment was so severe. Surely, she thought, the metal grazed the soft inner thighs of the victims when they walked. And how could they perform natural functions against such a rigid occlusion? Were they forbidden any sexual relief by their own hand or by the flesh of a lover?

"It isn't very nice, Bella, is it?" asked Paige, pressing her jewelled sex pad into Zacora's offered pouch.

Bella's chubby cheeks were sucked inwards and her nostrils flared as she watched her mistress pleasure the captive. "No," she hissed in frustration. "I'm only allowed to remove the block twice a day, and then I am watched to make sure that I do not pleasure myself."

Paige's scarlet lips kissed the captive's nipples, roving her tongue lovingly around each tight pink bud as she cupped the under swell with her gloved hands. The sensations were like nothing Zacora had felt before. They were mystical; transporting her to a realm where nothing had consequence apart from sexual pleasure. In this realm there were colours beyond the hues of the rainbow; there were enchanting scents. She tasted the food of the gods and she heard dulcet sounds that cossetted the ears. Her orgasm was not centred in her sex bud, but encompassed her whole body. Every centimetre of skin, every pore and every hair received a share of precious joy.

As she shuddered down from the elysian field Zacora felt Paige delving deep between her precious folds. The dark features of the other woman were tense with excitement; the nostrils flared on the slim nose, a smile curving the scarlet lips, the dark eyes glittering beneath dark and lowered lashes. The gloved hand first cupped the sex pouch, feeling its heat and fullness.

The touch, light and gentle though it was, made Zacora flush with shame. She was being tested like an animal on heat. The folds were parted with a finger and thumb, exposing an inflamed bud. Paige's fingers pinched this, stroking the moist little shaft from root to tip. In spite of the humiliation Zacora felt swirls of renewed excitement coursing around the inner flesh of her belly, making the nerves stretch to breaking point, but never quite reaching a peak.

She felt her head fall back, making the platinum tresses sway in soft curls against her naked back.

"I produce beautiful feelings for you, my darling, do I not?" breathed Paige, planting soft kisses on Zacora's exposed throat.

Zacora tried not to respond, but then two expert fingers were plunged into the cushiony wetness of her vagina. They were driven in to the hilt, leaving a thumb to play with the thrusting bud which jutted so eagerly from the gleaming bed of tender flesh.

The fingers drove in rhythmically causing the girl to arch backwards, the better to receive the forced attentions. "Oh, yes, my darling," hissed Paige, "don't hold back. Let the feelings flow over you like water from a warm spring."

Breasts full and tender, pouting upwards from her arched body, Zacora sighed her pleasure through lips circled to a perfect O. So great was her climax that her humiliation faded into the background of her mind.

Paige laughed as she slowly slid her fingers from the wildly fluttering sex folds. "Definitely, not so prim," she remarked, lifting the fingers to examine the moisture which gathered there. It lay on the black glove like pearls of dew gathered on the petals of a flower in the early morning. "A beautiful texture, my darling." Paige brought the fingers to her nose, sniffing the heady musk. "The aroma of a wood nymph," she said dreamily. The dark eyes became glazed for long moments as she allowed the scent to permeate her sensitive sinuses. "Are you sure you are human?" Paige's eyes became cautious and searching.

A weakness made the slender body of the captive slump in her ankle manacles, tumbling Zacora to the floor. The silver blonde hair flowed like a cloak around the fallen form, covering the creamy shoulders and allowing the women the merest glimpse of the full breasts.

"The orgasm was strong," said Paige kindly, "we must give her time to take her restitution." She placed the dewy fingers between her scarlet lips, tasting the coating left by the deep foraging into Zacora's depths. The expression on her face was thoughtful.

Bella cracked the soft strands of the lash she had chosen against her thigh. "She's stalling, mistress," she said pettishly.

"Perhaps you are right, Bella," replied Paige. She prodded Zacora with the toe of her boot. "Up you get, girl. No more of the play-acting."

Weakly, on trembling legs, Zacora got to her feet, cursing in her mind the shackles that held her fast to the stone floor. She kept her head bowed, not looking at either of the women, but hiding behind the billowing curtain of platinum hair.

Paige shrugged. "I think it is time for the punishment," she decided. "I know that there is something very special about you," she said softly, reaching into the curtain of hair to lift Zacora's chin, "and one day I shall discover it."

Bella, eager to begin the chastisement, spread Zacora's legs apart. The chains holding the captive's feet to the floor were loose enough for considerable width to be placed between the girl's shapely limbs.

"Yes, nice and wide, Bella," agreed Paige. "Open her up." She stroked the captive's full buttocks, feeling the satiny smoothness of the skin and the tautness of the athletic muscles.

Legs fully stretched, Zacora lifted her head, giving Paige a sapphire blue challenge with her proud eyes. She smiled a little as she saw the corsetted figure give a barely perceptible shudder.

"Hands flat on the ground," ordered Paige, trying to ignore Zacora's challenge. "We shouldn't wish you to fall and hurt yourself."

Once again Zacora was forced to submit to humiliating exposure of her perfect body. She knew that her rear mouth was fully revealed to the women. No doubt it was moist and pouting, but she hoped that it would not pulse and give them further satisfaction. She felt Paige's hands part her buttocks, examining that very orifice, circling it with the tip of her finger to test the flexibility of the puckered skin.

"No doubt the Prince will wish to plunder that further," the woman said, hissing her words cruelly. "He finds it stimulating to switch from one to the other of a woman's offerings. This one -" Paige probed the rear mouth with a finger still dewy with Zacora's pleasure juices "- so tight and gripping, and this one so flexible and slippery as silk," The fingers stroked the labia fluttering nervously across the girl's female entrance.

"A truly delicious sight," breathed Paige, standing back and allowing her eyes to stray up the long magnificent pillar of Zacora's splayed legs to the displayed silver fronded plump labia.

Paige made a careful inspection of the creamy bottom cheeks, stroking the stripes left by the soft lash. "Nicely swollen," she said, admiration in her voice, "but not welted." She took a moment to peer into the tangled mass of silver curls. "Hm," she murmured thoughtfully, "no tears. No expression either way. Perhaps a tinge harder next time, Bella."

The maid was only to happy to oblige. "Whatever you command, mistress. May I be so bold as to suggest a light slap in that open rear crevice to enhance the rosiness of the bud?"

Giving the maid a smile, Paige nodded, watching the operation with growing interest.

The victim gave another sigh; a deep intake of breath to relax her apprehensive nerve endings. The soft thongs of the whip were precisely placed, flicking the spread valley in which nuzzled the sensitive bud. Paige was delighted to see the bud purse at the soft caress of a lash. It began to pulse, seeming to reach out and grip the tip of the thong.

Zacora felt her pale face blush beneath the soft fall of the silken tresses and she gave up a silent plea that Paige would not notice the reaction, but her plea was in vain.

"You little darling!" Paige exclaimed. "The front slit is pearling nicely. And the clitoris is so delicately swollen, so full and engorged."

To her shame Zacora felt the maid's tiny hands smoothing the cream outwards into the silver forest of the labial growth. For all her meditation, her pleasure was revealed for the women. She felt herself rising up the inexorable slopes leading her to another crashing climax. Her mind pleaded for mercy but her buttocks and sex were posed for yet more punishment.

The shapely bottom presented itself, parted and ready for the next flourish of the caressing thongs. The moist labia, swollen and open, lifted obediently, the better to receive the benefit of the chastisement. Zacora, to her deep humiliation, felt her hot sap gathering on the already soaked silver bush. A trickle of the luscious juice made its way down a stately thigh. She could feel the urgent throb of her clitoris, projecting from her fluttering folds. It was jutting out of the tiny hood, begging for fulfilment.

"Oh, how pretty!" exulted Paige.

"Yes, mistress," agreed the maid, but Zacora knew that the serving wench was envious; wanted so badly to free her own sex from its dreadful metal prison.

"Won't the Prince just adore her?"

Zacora saw, through the lovely arch of her splayed thighs, that Paige's handsome swarthy face was inches from her fully revealed nether slit. The woman's hands, although not touching her flesh, were tracing each delicate curve. "Oh, you're so beautiful," Paige whispered. "And in a moment, when Bella has finished, I shall kiss you - there."

The tip of the gloved finger glanced across the naked tip of the glowing clitoris.

Zacora shuddered as she found herself bearing back towards Paige's softly parted scarlet lips. "Now, now!" she heard Paige chide, an amused chuckle whispering from the upturned mouth. "Patience, my little one. All good things come to those who wait. Carry on, Bella."

The supple thongs bore down again upon the offered flesh. They were placed, this time, so that they spread like a fan across all the posed parts. The blow was harder and Zacora stumbled forward a pace.

"That was hardly necessary, Bella," said Paige crossly. "You know perfectly well that she must not be damaged. Let me look at her skin."

Bella was pushed out of the way and Paige smoothed the welted buttocks, tracing each lash mark with gentle fingers. "If these bruise I shall have to deliver you for punishment to Freya and you know how she loves to give you maids the full treatment."

Zacora heard a harsh intake of fear from Bella.

"Now," continued Paige, ignoring Bella's show of apprehension, "continue, but I want the next strokes to be quicker."

Tears filled the sapphire blue eyes. Would her beatings never end? Zacora offered up a silent plea that the next stroke would touch her female bud which hovered so close to the brink of ecstasy. Humiliated by her position though she might be, she knew she must suffer the agony of the sexual appetite with which she had been cursed. But the thongs expertly skirted the pouting bud, leaving it jerking from the folds, untouched but begging.

"Enough," commanded Paige at last.

Zacora's buttocks were on fire. The normally pale flesh was swollen and each cheek was diverged from its natural position. She could feel her rear mouth pulsing, opening and closing as though urging intrusion. Juices were copious, drooling warmly down the inner skin of each lovely thigh. If only she was allowed to touch the heated bud probing from the silver folds her agony would be over, her climax would be instantaneous, but she knew that this was forbidden.

"Bring the stool," ordered Megan. The tremor in the woman's voice was ill-disguised. It told of sexual ardour and urgent need.

The glorious body which was the subject of this treatment trembled from head to foot. Zacora's need was almost unbearable. Always before she could meditate to close off pleasure and pain, but in this place every sensation seemed to be stronger.

The stool was placed in front of her. It was wide and quite high. The seat, if such it was, was fashioned from thick, hard leather.

"Bend over it," said Paige softly. Her breathing was rapid, Zacora noticed, harsh and laboured. Obediently, she did so.

The device was far more comfortable than merely bending over and clutching one's ankles. Her full breasts were free, peeping over the hard leather. It seemed only natural, as she rested on the leather, to part her legs to their fullest extent. The stool seemed to urge her to that position.

"Good girl!" praised Paige. "I wish all my pupils were so willing. Some of them are downright rebellious and some of them haven't a clue. But you, you are gorgeous, and I am about to reward you."

Breath, warm and needful, whispered over Zacora's offered flesh. Paige was blowing into the moist silver fronds, parting them gently with soft puffs. The sensation was delicately sensual and the girl performed appropriately, lifting the wet folds to increase their availability.

Knowing that her bud was Paige's goal, she concentrated upon that swollen knot. She had reached a point at which sexual satisfaction was the centre of her being. Nothing else mattered: not her humiliation, not her degradation, not being used like an object for the pleasure of others. She focused all her thoughts on her bud. Her sapphire blue eyes closed as she pictured Paige's object of desire in its inflamed bed of moist skin. She could see it, in her mind. She could see it growing, swelling, arching towards the questing scarlet lips through which darted an eager wet tongue.

"Yes, my darling," Paige sighed, "offer it to me nicely. Oh, oh, how it grows for me. How hot. You must do this for the Prince, my lovely."

At last Zacora felt Paige's lips around her clitoris. They sucked on it gently, caressing the little shaft. She felt an expert tongue press on the exposed tip and she felt that she would explode at the intent, but then the pressure was released and the gentle sucking of the shaft resumed. This alternate teasing and pleasuring continued until Zacora thought she would scream, but she refused to succumb. The only sign of her need was further opening of her legs and the faintest wiggle of her flushed bottom.

"Yes, I know," murmured Paige wetly, "you need release and I shall give it to you."

A leather-clad finger probed into the creamy depths of Zacora's folds. It stayed there, still and unmoving, until once more the girl could bear the delicious torture no longer. At last the soaking digit was withdrawn.

"Excellent!" praised Paige. "You have absolutely soaked it."

Zacora's body was flushed and heavy with sexual longing and she posed her nether parts, hoping that her torture would end. She felt her breasts swelling over the edge of the stool, the nipples burning and hard as stones, painful in their erection.

"Hold the buttock cheeks taut," ordered Paige of Bella. "Keep them fully open."

Bella was less than gentle in carrying out her mistress's bidding and Zacora felt true pain as the maid tugged at each fiery cheek. Warm wetness stroked around the victim's rear mouth. The entrance was thoroughly wetted before Paige was satisfied. The sap soaked finger was gently inserted and Zacora whispered a tiny sigh. At the same time Paige replaced her lips on the twitching bud amid the silver folds.

Almost immediately Zacora soared to new peaks, held there by Paige's undoubted expertise. The soaked finger drove in and out of the tight and clutching orifice. She felt degraded by this humiliating intrusion and her face burned with embarrassment, but this was as nought under the shadow of the ecstasy of her orgasm. She felt her liquid seeping from the silky folds, to gather on Paige's sucking lips. She felt her bud press deeper into the woman's mouth. She could feel its heat and the beautiful radiating sensation issuing to every part of her body.

Collapsing over the stool, Zacora was spent; taken to pleasure and beyond.

"I want you to pleasure me now," she heard with horror. From her commanded position on the stool she lifted her shimmering head to timorously glimpse round at her tormentors.

Paige, her scarlet lips shining with juices, had opened her black bush to reveal the dark tinted moistness beneath. A brown clitoris, with a red and glowing tip, jutted out, obviously very ready for stimulation. Zacora lowered her lovely head, shaking it vigorously in denial.

"You dare to disobey?" Paige's voice held threats of punishment too terrible to dream. The woman was on her feet, statuesque in the tightly boned corset, and her booted feet held wide apart ready for Zacora. The full breasts were swollen, the nipples glowing with heat. The gold rings twitched in the rigid flesh as Paige approached Zacora for the implied reward.

"Pull her to her feet, Bella," she commanded. "Place her mouth carefully. If she refuses to kiss my bud, use the whip."

"Of course, mistress," replied Bella, only too glad to oblige.

Satiated, Zacora was put to her task, but it wasn't through any sense of modesty or distaste that she had first refused to caress the dark beauty of Paige's sex.

The girl, kneeling, her lips parted and her sapphire eyes pleading, looked up at the older women. Her beautiful features begged that she should not be forced to close the satiny mouth around Paige's bud. She could smell the woman's heady musk; could see the swollen darkness of her folds; could see the urgent jerking redness of the clitoris.

It was beautiful, but Zacora must resist. She was determined to save the sexual energy which she might have to give for the man of her dreams. A man who could give her everything she wanted from life.

Zacora's pleading eyes travelled up the length of the leather clad legs. Silently, she begged that Paige should not compel her to caress the dark folds or suck the proud erection of her sex bud. How could she convey to her how much it meant to her to retain her sexual energy for the right man?

"What are you waiting for?" snapped Paige impatiently.

Bella stepped forward, eager to take up where she had left off.

The shimmering mane of silver hair shook vigorously from side to side as Zacora tried to communicate how important it was that she should not pleasure Paige.

"Oh, really!" hissed the induction mistress, seeing that her reluctance was serious. "You can take this prim and proper business too far, you know." Paige beckoned to Bella to hold the silver head and press it to her dark and parted nest.

No sooner was a hand placed in the thick depths of the gleaming hair than Zacora directed her beautiful eyes to Bella. She shrugged towards her, pointing at the several stranded whip, almost begging for it to be used on her crouching body. Her plaintive eyes then switched to Paige's black corsetted figure, so stately and strong.

"I do believe she wishes me to discipline her," smiled Paige. "What a strange girl she is!" The dark threatening beauty of the preparation mistress became more menacing. "You understand, my dear, that my thrashing will be beyond anything you have experienced?"

Zacora closed her lovely eyes, breathing deeply, smelling Paige's heavy musk as she crouched at the booted feet and nodded her acquiescence.

She heard the induction mistress groan pleasurably as she took the soft stranded whip from her maid. Zacora watched as Paige parted the darkness of her sex with her free hand, displaying the scarlet tipped clitoris.

The girl could see the slickness of the dark folds and the combined picture of Paige's sex and the anticipation of the lash brought startling stimulation to Zacora's whole body.

"Her needs are opening me up," breathed Paige huskily. "She does it much more daintily than you, or anyone else, for that matter."

"Yes, mistress," Bella rasped. She hated the way this witch was currying favour with her owner.

The captive lightly glanced at Paige's entrance, checking for the musky lubrication and the flexibility of the cushiony flesh.

Zacora's own flesh felt much the same. A lash, she thought, would be sufficient to bring her once more to orgasm.

"Don't they look lovely? Hers and mine?" whispered Paige. "One so dark and the other so pink and blonde?"

The lash snapped across the stone floor, touching nothing. What would it be like to caress a woman, thought Zacora? A picture formed in her mind, a picture of Paige bearing down on Zacora's own tantalising fingers. In the deeper recesses of her mind, the captive could see her own long tongue, pink and fleshy-looking, as it snaked through her wide, full lips. In Zacora's mind Paige watched it hungrily. What was more, the girl, in imagination, felt the darkly curled sex purse press forward and, suddenly, the tongue entered the spread heaven, probing into the moist leaves and delving into the cushiony passage.

The two women merged in mind and body.

"Is she really touching me?" breathed Paige, disbelief in her voice. "It feels like a sex sword. It's thick and long. Oh, it's so lovely and so strange. Wonderful." The words came out hesitantly, as though the woman was in the throes of a climax.

The captive girl allowed her tongue and her mind to relax and slip softly out of the deep, pulsing pit. She transferred her attentions to the jerking hard reality of Paige's bud.

Soon a groan, long and loud, escaped from her. "I've never felt anything so wonderful," Paige told Bella. "What is she doing which causes such thrills?" Again the voice was hesitant, breathless.

"Nothing that I can see, mistress," said Bella, frowning. "But your clitoris hood is bared at the tip and it waves from side to side as though lightly brushed with a tongue across the scarlet flesh - just as I would do, should I be allowed."

Another groan, louder this time, filled the induction chamber. "You'll have to stop," pleaded Paige. "It's too wonderful - too beautiful - too much." She was swaying weakly, fingering the inflamed and erect nipples of her exposed breasts. Her eyes were lifted, rolling in their sockets as she bore down on the imagined magic of Zacora's tongue

Paige's sex bud was greatly enlarged and the girl began to physically caress it with lips as soft as swansdown, while her tongue lapped the engorged tip.

Heat diffused from the lapping tongue, seeping into the cossetted flesh. The wonder of the sensations she was causing were reflected back to Zacora and she smiled to herself. She knew that Paige could not take much more. It would be very soon.

Sex sap, warm and creamy, dripped steadily into Zacora's throat and she could hear Paige's breathing, quick and harsh. She played her long tongue around the base of the clitoris stem, feeling it throb and jerk. Next she pressed further to ease back the tiny hood and finally, she poised for a final touch of the tip.

Paige gave a great roar of pleasure and she fell to the floor, her black-booted legs folded under her body so that her ebony nest was thrust high. "Beautiful," she repeated over and over again. "Beautiful."

Concerned, Bella knelt by her mistress, her hands fluttering at her chastity bar as if to infiltrate the barrier. "Mistress Paige," she said softly, "are you well?"

Zacora, her face gleaming with silvery juices from the induction mistress's sex purse, knelt with her head bowed. Her body glowed with the sweat of exertion. Her mind, too, was weary. She felt a hand grip a handful of silver tresses to lift her head back. That done she felt a sharp slap across her bare breasts; first one tender mound and then the other.

"What have you done to my mistress?" hissed Bella angrily into Zacora's pale face.

The captive shrugged, raising her hands in pretend innocence. She pointed to the feet manacles, indicating that she wanted release.

"If I release you, will you tell me?"

Zacora nodded eagerly.

Paige held her pouting sex, cupping it lovingly as she murmured her litany of "Beautiful." She was a sensual sight. Her naked breasts were swollen and her voluptuous figure was tightly encased in the black corset. Any man entering the induction room would wish to spear her with his sex sword, but Zacora's mind games caused a madness which would repel potential marauders.

The bandaged feet free at last, Zacora sped for the heavy oak door. Bella was close behind her, grabbing the willowy girl by her most tender parts, but Zacora, lithe and supple, slipped out of the clumsy grasp as if she had been lubricated with butter.

"You won't get away with this!" she heard as she leapt like a gazelle down the long passage. Even with tender, torn feet Zacora had the easy stride of an athlete.

CHAPTER THIRTEEN

"Ah, Bernlada," greeted the Prince cordially.

Elegant in bright yellow satin robes, His Highness lounged on his opulent padded throne. "We've been expecting you these many minutes past." His voice was deep and cultured and his finely sculpted face smiled at the dark little woman who served him so well.

Still cupping her naked sex purse Bernlada managed a deep curtsy which displayed her dark folds prettily. "My apologies, Highness. I had reason to escort Callan to the punishment mistress and this delayed me."

The beautifully drawn dark eyebrows arched in surprise and the eyes widened. "Callan brought to Freya? Why so?"

Warm spume oozed through Bernlada's fingers. "Please, your Highness, may I relay the report to you later. I am losing Callan's issue which is so important to your treatment." Added to which, she thought, I don't want to incur your wrath.

Bernlada loved the throne room. How she would have adored to bear the Prince's child. What a good Queen she would have surely made.

The floor was strewn with satin cushions in hues as brilliant as a strutting peacock. The walls were hung with silken embroideries depicting couples entwined in every position of the act of copulation. Horned satyrs took nymphs in woodland glades, expressions of outright lust suffusing their animal-like features. The nymphs, beautiful and delicate, took all intrusions in ecstatic eagerness. Imps climbed oiled phalluses of gigantic proportions and prepared to thrust these magnificent organs into cavernous fleshy gateways.

More imps caressed sperm sacs at the bases of the trunk-like genitals, as if urging them to produce oceans of semen.

"The hangings always inspire you, don't they Bernlada?" The Prince's pale eyes glinted with pleasure as he watched his sex servant look around the room.

"Oh, yes Highness." Bernlada turned admiring eyes on the Prince. His tightly tailored satin suit emphasised the darkness of his skin. She loved the way his dark eyes contrasted with his brown muscular body.

His suit had a tight vest which emphasised the magnificent pectorals and narrow waist. The well-cut breeches skimmed over his slim hips and clung to the honed thighs and calves. His feet were shod in matching yellow slippers, decorated with precious stones. On his black curly hair there was a crown, simple but elegant.

She sank to her knees, paying homage to her sovereign, freeing his penis with trembling fingers so that it sprang erect, probing towards her moist lips. She adored him as a wife adores a loving husband. Lustrous dark eyes fixed upon the naked object of her desire she admired the satin smoothness of the brown stem. She felt her mouth become wet at the thought of caressing the thick globe with her tongue. The circumcised end bulb gleamed purple in the softly lit throne room and peeped at her through its wide single eye. She felt her breasts become painfully full at the sight, and felt her sex bud jerk in the pool of Callan's spume in the carefully closed pouch.

The Prince placed an affectionate hand in her wild curly hair, stroking the ebony tresses. "I love your frolicsome little ways, Bernlada," he said in his deep, gracious voice. "I cannot resist your wiles. Place those soft lips of yours around the royal fullness and give it the gentlest of kisses." He paused and lifted her dainty chin, forcing her to look up at him. "But remember you must not take whatever potency may be in my cockshaft. It is for the maiden found upon the woodland path."

"Of course, your Highness," she said, in a strained tight voice. To her the Prince's penis was as sacred as any sceptre. She wanted it buried in her to the hilt; she wanted him to spray his spume into her vessel; wanted him to be entirely potent. Caressing it with her lips was not what she wanted, but she knew it would have to suffice, understood that he must save his seed for the captive, for the child to be.

"A tongue to charm a stone phallus," she heard. The Prince sighed the words as he pressed his crisply curled pubis forward for Bernlada's attentions. His shaft swayed before her eyes, the purple shining globe brushing her ready lips. She gave him a warm smile. He looked so magnificent, looming above her, his hands at his waist as he thrust forward; a golden clothed god.

Cupping his heavy bulbs in one dainty hand, she made her lips soft and flexible. The undertaking must be carried out delicately so as not to incur any release of his Highness's precious issue. The globe only was enclosed in the moistness and warmth of her mouth. Tenderly, she kneaded beyond the neatly cut globe, to engulf just a fraction of his stem. It felt smooth, hot and thick against her velvety lips. Her tongue found the deep pit of the Prince's eye and she caressed it, probing into the salty moistness, to taste the first issue of royal juices.

"How goes the induction?" asked the Prince conversationally. "Has Morgan begun the preparation?"

Bernlada continued to caress the proudness of the Prince's globe. She could have nodded her acquiescence to both questions, but she chose to avoid answering.

The Prince placed both his hands on her curls, pressing the groin to her face. "Of course," he said lightly, "you cannot speak for the moment." She felt his slim, athletic hips gyrate slowly and rhythmically. He was obviously enjoying her attention. "I can't wait to embed myself in those silver fronds," he added hoarsely.

Fierce tension strung Bernlada's small body to a mass of angry sinews.

"I am sure that she will produce my son before the year is out," breathed the Prince. "Wouldn't it be wonderful if she conceived tonight?" The thickening end globe thrust excitedly between Bernlada's willing lips.

Continue, my Prince, continue, thought Bernlada happily, and the issue will be used, whether it is potent or not. I shall receive it, savour it, drink it and it will be mine.

"From whence does she come?" added the Prince dreamily. "With that colouring she is not of our lands. She really is very special, is she not?"

The searching tongue dipped greedily into the royal pit, inserting itself to open the entrance to the sperm passage. A cossetting hand stroked the firm issue banks, rolling them in their sacs, feeling them draw up with pleasurable tension.

"There's a magical quality about her, don't you think?" The Prince was, unknowingly, urging Bernlada's excitation of his sex as he thought of the nymph he found in the glade. "There's an aura. She simmers as one looks into those deep sapphire pools. She has cast a spell on me, I am sure."

This last remark was too much for Bernlada. Her sharp even teeth grated upon the tenderness of the Prince's sex sword as she withdrew her mouth from his globe.

He looked at her in hurt surprise. Bernlada had always been the tenderest of servants, treating his cock with the reverence that a princely staff deserved.

"You wished me not to cause your spume to gush before you meet Miss Prim; before you spread her upon the coupling throne." Bernlada spilled out the words hastily to explain her roughness. The dark little slave gestured towards the specially designed throne which thrust the subject's pubis in such a position that it became a receptacle for hot, spurted issue. There were stirrups in which the subject's legs were placed to hold them widely splayed. The arms, too, were held together above the subject's head, to thrust the breasts high and available, should His Highness wish to avail himself of the suckling.

"Yes," nodded the Prince. "Quite right." Nevertheless, he cradled his cock gingerly, nursing it back to full stature.

"Allow me, your Highness," Bernlada said with a smile. "Let it be part of your treatment. They are preparing her for you. She must be nearly ready now."

The Prince hesitated, not quite trusting her. "Very well then," he agreed at last. "But gentle, if you please."

"Yes, Highness, whatever pleases you." Bernlada's voice dripped molasses.

The Prince preened, thrusting his mighty staff forward to receive the treatment. Quite recovered from the nip of Bernlada's sharp teeth, the brown shaft glimmered with the sheen left by her lips. He posed the swollen globe, a shining purple weapon with such an aura of power. "Why will it not bear fruit?" he mused sadly, his handsome features softened by emotion.

"Always the wrong partner, Highness." Bernlada was terse in her observation.

"Indeed, yes," he agreed. "But with this girl it will be different!"

Bernlada squatted, opening her smooth coffee-coloured limbs wide and bending her knees. Slowly, she opened her sex purse, spreading the fat lips with their thick ebony curls. The Prince watched her as she tilted the pouch forward, displaying the dripping folds with their swollen bud jerking in a tantalising rhythm.

"Oh, sweet girl," he murmured, his voice husky with excitement, "would that you were of noble birth."

Bernlada ignored his words, concentrating on stimulating all of his senses. Her small fingers delved into her wet chasm, seeking out every droplet of Callan's issue. Smiling, she held out the treasure in her cupped hand. It shimmered like a great liquid pearl, seething with life. It issued tendrils of vaporous heat, and she held the steaming jewel close to the Prince's nose. His eyes closed as the hearty male musk enfolded his senses. The aroma made his genitals enlarge again, grow harder and more vigorous.

"Callan is magically potent, sire," whispered Bernlada.

"Yes," breathed the Prince, his eyes transfixed on the liquid globule cupped in the woman's hand. Splay legged he shuffled closer, offering himself to Bernlada.

Vapour curled around the Prince's thick, probing shaft, caressing it and cossetting the firm sacs nestling darkly against the yellow silk. With a swift movement of her dextrous hands she swamped the purple globe with the carefully conserved fluid.

A pleasured sigh escaped the Prince's full lips as the heat of the globule seeped into the fine dark skin. Bernlada massaged the slickness along the whole length of the offered royal shaft. As she continued to caress she felt the girth increase until it was necessary to use both her small hands to encircle the thickness.

"Yes, it has magical properties, Callan's spume," the Prince whispered. His lean dark body was arched backwards and his eyes were closed as he luxuriated in Bernlada's attention.

"Indeed, Highness," agreed the girl, but she knew that it was her sensual touch which worked the magic. It was the rhythmic slide of her tiny fingers up and down the silky, rigid length and the light flick upon the magnificently swollen end globe at each trail from tip to base. She slid one hand down beneath the gracefully hung sacs to that sensitive spot between them and the royal bottom mouth. The pad of a finger pressed lightly at that rigid place. The Prince groaned with pleasure, tending his massive erection.

"I regret that I cannot allow you to have a child by this," he said, opening his eyes to admire the shining stem towering from his groin. He tested its bursting thickness by attempting to circle his thumb and finger around it. The digits did not meet and he gave a satisfied nod.

Bernlada bit her lips to hold back the gasp of horror which she caught, just in time, in her throat. "Pray do not trouble your royal mind," she begged. She had other plans for her womb; important plans. It was just a question of timing.

Pleasantly relaxed from Bernlada's massage, the Prince walked unhurriedly to the coupling throne. "Go to Morgan," he said huskily, "tell her to bring the girl before me." His large dark eyes closed once more, the lashes thick and lush upon the dusky cheeks. The wide lips were gently parted, showing strong white teeth. Indeed, thought Bernlada, the Prince was the handsomest of men.

Her thoughts fluttered to Callan, her partner for so many changes of the moon. Yes, he was handsome too, but in a more brutal manner than the Prince. She felt she could manage the Prince with ease. He was gentle and it would be easy to make him love her. Her mind was made up.

"What if Miss Prim does not wish to come to the royal presence?" she suggested quietly.

The Prince's eyes snapped open. "Does not wish?" he repeated disbelievingly. "Does not wish?" He stroked his staff nervously, as if expecting it to wilt or disappear.

"She is not called Miss Prim for nought, your Highness," reminded Bernlada mischievously.

"Of course she will wish to come," He dismissed any other possibility. "By the time Morgan has finished her induction the maid will be ready for me. She will wish to have me over and over again. Morgan has prepared frigid virgins for me and the coupling has been most successful." His dark face became sad as he remembered. "But still they did not bear me sons."

"Quite, your Highness," said Bernlada triumphantly.

"But the silver maid has a special quality." The Prince's eyes gleamed with hope. "Morgan assures me so."

"If you say so, your Highness. I shall relay the message that the maid is required for the coupling throne."

"Now!" thundered the Prince. "Now whilst I am in the mood!"

"Yes Sire." Bernlada even walked out of the throne room backwards. This act of respect was one with which she normally would not bother. Her privileged position as sex slave excused her from that duty. But she knew that the Prince delighted in her small voluptuousness, so she preened her beauty. Taking very slow, swaying steps she reversed from his presence, taking pains to pose her full breasts and lushly curled mound as she faded from his view.

Watching him, from the far end of the magnificent throne room, she saw his eyes flare with passion; saw his hand raise as though to beckon her to return, but she merely cupped the soft fullness of her breasts, as if in a gesture of farewell, and slipped through the ornate gilded doors and she was gone.

CHAPTER FOURTEEN

Zacora sped this way and that, along narrow corridors with many doors on each side; along wide passages, some with gracious hangings and some with panels.

Gingerly, she opened a door. The room before her was huge, stretching into the distance...

A strong muscular arm reached out of the chink she had created by opening the door. Her willowy wrist was grabbed in a grip of iron and she was pulled through. Her sapphire eyes widened in terror. Again she was captured, this time held fast by a man so vast that she must strain her neck to see his eyes and so broad that her long, slim arms could not encircle his huge frame.

He was a giant.

"Bring her to me, Mapoto." The voice came from the far end of the room; from a man huddled in a pile of satin cushions, so richly hued that it hurt Zacora's eyes to look at them. "She is the one for whom we have been waiting."

Zacora realised that this was the Prince; the one to whom she was to be given. Sadness cloaked her lovely body. She had been seeking Callan. Callan would have helped her.

The giant, Mapoto, picked her up with one arm, circling her waist to carry her to the Prince.

"Not like that!" said the sovereign. "You will damage her. Hold her in both arms."

The giant looked crestfallen as he gently cradled her across his arm, stroking her firm and beautifully rounded breasts with a finger.

The ground looked very far away as Zacora looked down. She shivered with fear. If only she had not opened that particular door. There were so many others which she could have chosen. She felt the giant fingers stroking the pronounced curves of her bottom, parting the cheeks. A huge finger slipped to her moist front cleft and Zacora wriggled in alarm.

"What are you doing, Mapoto?" The Prince's voice showed the depth of his anger.

Zacora could see the Prince quite clearly now. A handsome man, dressed in a golden yellow suit.

"In any case she could not accommodate you," said the Prince. "You would split the poor little soul."

Mapoto placed Zacora next to the Prince, letting her sink into the downy cushions. Although the giant let her slip down as gently as he could, she still fell several feet and her arms and legs splayed gracefully apart.

Zacora tried to arrange herself more decorously on the silken cushions, but the Prince stopped her. "Stay just as you are," he ordered with a smile. "You look so very lovely like that." His dark soft hand reached out to stroke the arms which were flung above her head. This position thrust her breasts upwards, as if they were on offer to him.

The same hand had traced her long slender legs, bent at the knee and spread outwards. He sighed with sheer delight when he saw the silver wisps of her nest, parted to reveal the deep pink of the folds and proud erection of her bud. His eyes slid down to her sorely used feet, to the bandages which were loose and patched with scarlet blood spots.

"But you have not been properly prepared for me." The Prince's smile of admiration changed to an angry frown. "What is Paige thinking of to send you to me in this condition?"

At the mention of Paige's name, Zacora immediately became tense and aware, ready for trouble.

"You should be swathed in gossamer, as fine and transparent as a spider's web," the Prince continued. "It should be draped across the delicate mounds of your breasts, to merely lift, but not hide. Each nipple should be clasped in gold rings, set with precious stones, to stimulate the rosy erection and to make you feel very special."

The Prince's wide soft lips caressed each nipple and then his sharp white teeth grated the tender flesh, to emulate the feel of the clamps. Zacora tried to lower her arms but she was prevented. Mapoto held her wrists with his finger and thumb, using his other hand to bind her slender upper limbs with a silken cord.

The Prince returned to stroking her splayed thighs, but he was still distracted. "What shall we do about Paige?" A frown marred the royal features.

Zacora shook her head, tumbling the silver tresses from side to side, spraying the myriad of colours in the cushions with spun threads of platinum and gold.

"Nothing?" laughed the Prince. "Surely not. She should be sent to the dungeons to take some of Freya's medicine."

Zacora's hair shook more wildly. The last thing she wanted was Paige's madness discovered.

"Kind and thoughtful as well as beautiful," remarked the Prince. His soft touch grazed up her splayed thighs until he reached the lushness of the spun silver nest. She flinched away and he laughed lightly. "Miss Prim, of course! Your name quite slipped my mind." He looked into the wide sapphire eyes, allowing his gaze to linger deep in the blue pools. Zacora saw him shudder, as though he saw something which caused great fear. He looked away from the pale, beautiful face which held so many secrets.

"This..." His finger traced, but did not touch, the perfection of her nether regions. "This should be draped in gossamer veils, looped lightly through a jewelled belt. Such a garment would cover, but leave each orifice available for my touch when I require it." He smiled at her. The fear had faded from his fine features and Zacora could see lust in his dark eyes. "Would you like me to pleasure you? Shall I place you on a coupling throne?" His voice became wistful. "Will you give me an heir?"

Zacora, her hands bonded above her head, was helpless. All of her life she had searched for someone who would take care of her, but all she received was humiliation.

The Prince's dark eyes hardened. "Place her on the coupling throne, Mapoto. Let us have no more delay."

An uncontrollable shiver took over Zacora's slender body as she watched the giant approach her. He was fully twelve feet tall. His massive upper body was decorated with tattoos depicting serpents and dragons interspersed with maidens being defiled by giants like himself.

He pointed proudly to a cockshaft of massive girth and length, sliding into a maiden, not dissimilar to Zacora in appearance. The maid looked ecstatic, even though the stem which pierced her was taking her life. "In my home," he said in a deep, booming voice, "that is the custom."

Zacora's shivering became more violent, but she could not resist looking at Mapoto's crotch. His sex sword, perhaps for the best, was sheathed in a golden cod piece which decorated silken trousers, loose and baggy, but gathered at his ankles.

The giant swept her up, gently this time, but the arm which held her lower body slipped between her thighs, grazing her soft sex and holding her legs wide open. A great tattooed hand, the size of a dish which would hold a Christmas turkey with ease, caressed the shuddering firmness of her breasts. The same hand held her arms above her head. The giant's grip was firm, but gentle, almost sensual.

"The coupling throne," reminded the Prince, jumping lithely to his feet and following his giant bodyguard to the fearsome looking seat on the dais at the far end of the chamber. He stroked it, feeling its silky perfection, kept in daily trim by Bernlada's ministrations.

Zacora watched him warily from her high vantage, casting the sapphire eyes at the tawny shaft with its gleaming globe. It was, she had to admit, a handsome weapon, but there was something about the Prince which told her that he was not a fitting sovereign.

There was a weakness, a lack of potency in him. There was a softness about the finely sculpted features; a lack of certainty about his manner.

The small procession reached the coupling throne. Mapoto looked at the Prince questioningly.

"Place the wrist bonds over this hook." The Prince pointed to a golden peg on the back of the chair and Zacora knew that her arms would be stretched to the limit and her breasts lifted painfully once she was captured on the throne.

"Yes, master," intoned the giant. The slender arms were placed in position and the silk bonds slipped over the peg. Mapoto released his hold on Zacora and her long legs dangled freely. She was suspended from the peg. The pain in her shoulders was excruciating, and yet, hanging there, a strange freedom entered her silver fronded pouch. Her sex sap flowed freely, drooling over the silver fronds and down the creamy thighs. Her clitoris jutted clear of the swollen lips.

Zacora's arms ached dreadfully, but all the time her sex became more moist, softer and more willing. Not for the Prince, she assured herself. Her thoughts flew more and more to Callan. The leather loincloth which lifted at the sight of her to show the rigid magnificence of his male shaft; that was the picture which was in the forefront of her mind.

She felt the Prince's hands on the cushioned firmness of her bottom cheeks, placing them in the narrow saddle-like platform. His long, soft fingers lingered at the depth of her buttock cleft, spreading the deep valley open. With a cajoling smile he slipped each ankle in turn into soft leather stirrups, tightening buckles around her bandaged limbs.

She knew that she was fully open to him. That he could see every fold and every moist crevice. She knew that her silver fronds were shining with pearls of sex dew. There should have been pride in her mind for all her training had led to such a moment as this, but the Prince, though noble, was not the man for her.

Her needs were for a stricter, stronger man. A man who could tame her naturally rebellious nature.

"Prepared or not," breathed the Prince, "you are a stimulating sight."

Zacora lowered her eyes, only too aware of her openness, her availability. She felt that she was sacrificed on the alter of a god of potency.

"Look at me," begged the Prince. His golden clad legs were straddled directly in front of her. He was holding his rigid staff with both hands, offering it to her, like some tasty morsel. Zacora licked her soft lips, letting the tip of her skilled tongue rove around the deliciously fine skin.

His eyes strayed to the velvety slickness of the folds of her pouch. His dark eyes glinted with naked lust. So piercing was his gaze that she could almost feel it touching the dew which pearled on the folds. She knew that he was focusing on her swollen bud, alive with his erection, its tip bared.

The Prince groaned as he approached the throne, poising his globe to enter her helpless body.

"NO!"

It was a loud shout from the opening door.

Mapoto turned and growled, striding towards the speaker with thunderous steps, his great footfalls echoing through the vast chamber.

Zacora saw a being, hooded with tight black leather and dressed in a skin-tight black body suit which clothed him totally. At the crotch there was a metal guard, a codpiece, large, cone shaped and shiny. The intruder was wielding a great two-handed sword which he slashed from side to side, parrying Mapoto away. His skill was such that it was inevitable that the ponderous giant would be felled.

Uncertain who the intruder might be, Zacora hung, imprisoned and passive, on the great throne. Was she to be set free? Was the rescuer Harold the Pretender, thunderously angry at his expensive loss?

Her gaze shifted limpidly to the Prince's dark face so close to hers. He was terrified. The expression of fear was frozen on his handsome features. The once rigid shaft was softening at her warm, moist entrance, folding like a sleeping serpent into a soft coil.

Zacora's rescuer, if such he was to be, stormed forward over the fallen Mapoto, who lay like a great felled tree in a fast spreading pool of blood. How had Mapoto been overcome? In the confusion she had missed this feat, but the newcomer had a great sword in his hands and Mapoto, huge though he was, had been unarmed.

Supple black leather, a full length suit covering the stranger from toes to fingertips, lay upon his muscular body like a second skin. All that could be seen of his face were the dark, glittering eyes and the mouth, sensuous but firm.

The Prince was flung from Zacora's pliant body and the sword was used to split the silken bond that held her wrists to the chair. Wide sapphire eyes looked up at the black clad stranger, thanking him with parted, mute lips. Now the stirrups of the coupling throne were slashed and Zacora was free, pulled to her feet. She winced and she was immediately lifted tenderly into the stranger's arms as he ran from the room.

The last she saw of the Prince was a writhing heap of misery at the foot of the now useless coupling throne, wailing and beating upon the floor with both fists.

As for the fugitives, nothing passed between them for many minutes. The man loped easily along the network of passageways with his slender burden in his arms and his sword resheathed at his side.

"A horse awaits at the palace gates," he said at last, hardly breathless in spite of his exertions.

Zacora smiled up at him, leaning the tumbled platinum tresses on his broad chest and feeling comfort by his arms. The strength, the muscular body, these things spoke of Harold.

They sped across a narrow bridge which spanned the moat surrounding the palace. A splendid white charger pawed the ground in a small copse close by. With apparent ease he slid her onto the saddle before swinging up behind her.

The thought of Harold holding her close against his splendid body brought her bud to full erection against the cold of the saddle. Juices poured from her opening, creating a dark patch on the tawny leather. He had come for her. Come for her alone. There was no sign of his horrible Aunt or her diabolical son. Her life, she felt was complete.

"Shall I place you sideways in the saddle?" he queried softly, concern for her comfort plain in his voice.

She shook the silver and gold curls, her head bowed subserviently.

He looped the reins in his hand and Zacora felt the fine leather of his sleeve brush both her breasts as he urged the horse gradually into a gallop.

"In the forest," he said, "there is an abandoned cottage. We can rest there for the night."

Before returning to your castle, she thought. Had he told those awful relatives of his to go?

The rhythmic movement under her crotch stimulated Zacora. In her belly was a swirling maelstrom of heaviness, hot and weighty, pressing down on her most sensitive parts. She leaned back, luxuriating in the feeling. Her eyes closed and her soft lips parted. Her rescuer pinched the delicate flesh of her nipples, flicking them until tiny frissons of pleasurable pain fluttered down her body.

One of his leather gloved hands reached down to part her folds, allowing the cold evening air, moved by the swift progress of the horse, to enter the heat and moisture of the delectable entrance. Zacora wriggled pleasurably, wanting to give him delights such as he had never known.

"Be still," he chuckled. "There will be time later."

The voice sounded strange; not as she remembered it, but that, she told herself, was because of the leather hood. The body was strong and the touch on her body was sensual, in spite of the tightly fitting gloves.

The hand holding the reins also held a breast, cupped softly and tweaking the tautness of the nipple. The other hand spread her eager folds, abrading the clitoris with one finger while the middle finger delved deeply into the darkness of her well. Zaeora rode the delicious rapture as she soared from peak to peak.

She slumped forward in the saddle, her long soft curls covering the pale fullness of her breasts, exhausted by the events of the day. It would have been better to remain in the castle, endure Megan and Gareth and, perhaps, gradually cajole Harold to asking them to leave her alone.

She could feel the odd swelling of the rigid codpiece which covered his glorious maleness. It dug into the cleft of her buttocks, parting them. His breathing was rapid and she could feel the heat of his breath on her neck where he swept the silken coils of hair over her creamy shoulders.

"We have some way to go," he told her, "before we reach the cottage."

Zacora nodded disconsolately as they galloped along the forest path.

"Would you like to hear how I escaped from the dungeons?"

Her heart lurched. The dungeons? Why was Harold in the dungeons?

"How I came to be in this ridiculous suit?"

Zacora half-turned in the saddle, looking into the slits of the mask; looking into the depths of the eyes. Callan! It was Callan, not Harold. Her heart sank.

"Quite a story," he said, holding her more tightly. "Freya, the punishment woman, drugged me, and when I woke I was dressed in this suit and splayed in a torture chair."

Zacora made no comment. Her thoughts were with Harold. Would he, indeed, come to look for her?

The night was coming. The two suns of Vakir sank simultaneously, making the sky blood red in both directions. The trees of the forest, silhouetted against the darkening sky, seemed to be cut from black card and stuck to a scarlet backdrop. As the suns set it became colder and Zacora snuggled against Callan.

"My rampant beast was her undoing."

Zacora sighed. Callan's bragging tone was boring her. She wanted Harold, who would take her without all this talk of his magnificence.

"I persuaded her to loose me so that we could place my devil where it belonged. It wasn't long before she released me after that, I can tell you." He gave a triumphant laugh and Zacora gave an almost imperceptible sigh. "I gave her a taste of her own medicine. Had her clamped in the chair before she knew what hit her."

Zacora gave him a bored smile.

"The cottage is just ahead." She gave a horrified gasp at the sight of the old dwelling. It was tumbledown and half hidden in an overgrown garden. Callan dismounted and turned to lift Zacora from the charger. "We'll rest here for the night," he said, holding her clasped in his arms, "and decide our plans tomorrow."

He did not see her grimace of distaste. She knew her plans for the morrow did not include him, not if she could help it.

CHAPTER FIFTEEN

The search was going badly and Megan was out of breath and thoroughly out of sorts. Her favourite hat, the black one with the wide brim and the high pointed crown, was dusty and crumpled, her long brown hair mussed and tangled.

"There's a cottage beyond the rise ahead." she said to Gareth, who was lagging behind. "We'll check there. If no-one has seen or heard of her, we'll camp there for the night and go on in the morning... but look - surely there's smoke above the trees?"

She began a stealthy approach and soon they both were peering through a dirty window.

Sure enough, there were silver curls spread upon a pile of animal skins. Zacora's sapphire eyes were closed.

The cottage was lit by a single candle. Someone seemed to have given the girl clothes. Megan snarled angrily. She liked her favourite slave to be naked and totally available. Still, she consoled herself, the clothing was very brief.

A dress stitched roughly from a striped skin covered one full breast. The other was as bare as ever; full and pouting with the pink nipple erect. The skirt of the rough dress was brief, not covering the sex pouch. Wisps of silver curls escaped beneath the skin. A belt cinched the narrow waist and it was made from plaited vines.

Zacora moved, easing her long legs provocatively open. Megan could see the silver wisps gleam in the flickering light of the candle. They were moist; that was obvious. Mistress Meleagan frowned, but licked her lips as she savoured the memory of the girl's taste. She'd had her where she wanted her then.

Something moved in the shadows. A man! He was tall, broad and devilishly good looking, from what they could see of him, which wasn't much. He was dressed in black, black leather. His cock was bare, however, spearing towards the girl's widening legs.

Zacora was raising her buttocks.

"In!" she ordered. "Quick! Get her!"

Megan was already filling the doorway with her considerable girth, preparing to approach the couple in the cottage. "I've got the ropes," she breathed cheerfully.

In spite of his strength Callan was no match for the skilled ropemanship of the two Meleagans. He and Zacora were soon trussed at ankles and wrists, their slim bodies arched backwards. Gareth fondled the girl's naked breast, squeezing the nipple between his first and second fingers. He felt her wince as his teeth grated the tender flesh, but it also became more erect.

"You love it, don't you?" he whispered.

"She hates it!" gritted Callan.

"Gag this one," ordered Megan. She turned to Zacora, gazing down at her bound vulnerability as rag was jammed into Callan's mouth. How she loved to fondle Zacora's moistness, spread her folds to fully expose her pink clitoris. She turned to the slave's bound lover to trail her fingers along his smooth erection.

Megan had a string of beads round her smooth her neck. She was playing with them thoughtfully, looking at Callan's thickness. The globe was already moist, gleaming in the soft, flickering light. The eye drooled a pearly drop of dew, in spite of the pain which her tight trussing must have caused him.

She smiled as she unfastened the necklace, letting the beads trail through her hands slowly. "Roll her on to her stomach, Gareth," she ordered. Gareth obeyed, keeping a pleased eye on Zacora's bare buttocks peeping from the brief dress. They looked pale, firm and very enticing as the slave rocked on the dirt floor of the cottage.

The beads were dangled before the sapphire eyes. "Do you know what I'm going to do with these, my sweet?"

Zacora's eyes widened and her lips parted. The mouth was so enticing; so open, so ready.

Gareth's sex weapon was heavy in his hand. He stroked the rigid member, caressing the silky skin and smoothing its own dew from the globe and along its own length.

Zacora nodded, showing that she knew exactly what was to be done to her. It was humiliating, but her pleasure always soared readily when it was time.

Her bound lover watched, his dark eyes angry, and yet there was another expression, excitement. He, too, knew what was to be done to the arched girl.

Megan gently stroked the smooth round beads through the hot moistness of the silver female cleft. The bound slave felt the beads judder over her hard bud over and over again. Zacora felt her eyes close with the lethargy of need; felt her body go heavy and molten from the inside.

Her open mouth was suddenly plundered with the thickness of Gareth's weapon, filling her throat. It wasn't an unpleasant feeling, even though he was rather rough; probing back and forth to the very depths of her throat.

"He loves to watch," chuckled Megan, referring to Callan. "We must do something about that." She took a device from the belt around the suit of armour. It was a codpiece of chain mail to be fixed around the wearer with a padlock.

Callan was not in a position to struggle. His throbbing sex weapon was rigid with excitement and the fit in the codpiece was far from easy. His eyes widened as the devilish device was fitted around his sac and the stiff length of his flesh.

"There," she said, sitting back with an expression of satisfaction on her face. She could see the straining flesh through the mesh of the chain, calling to mind a caged serpent.

Zacora's eyes were hooded as she soared to her climax, ready to take the hot, creamy issue to be poured into her throat. Gareth was pumping into her hard.

As the girl soared up and up the slicked beads were placed one by one into her rear mouth. Megan was watching carefully; watching the pulsing of the sex folds, watching the throbbing clitoris.

It was time. Megan knew by the juices pouring from the pink folds. She quickly popped the beads from the rear mouth, from the clenching sphincter and, deliciously, she plunged a finger into the creaming front entrance.

Gareth grunted, saturating Zacora. He spilled over her lips and she allowed it to trickle like a pearly stream down her chin and neck.

Zacora was humiliated, but when she looked at Harold, she knew that it did not matter. He found it stimulating to see her pleasure thus.

Megan sighed, kneeling with her fine plump thighs well splayed. Her short dress, the black silk dusty now from the rough floor, was hitched to her bare wide patch. She felt her own well developed nubbin become very urgent.

She looked at Zacora. The girl was a delicious plaything; so passive and pliant, almost eager to be humiliated, and yet she had run away, and, as a result, they had to spend the night in this dreary cottage.

Taking off her hat, Megan lay, disgruntled and splay legged, hands delving for comfort into the moist heat of her nest. Each forefinger pressed open the pouting thickness of the lips. Each second finger splayed the swelling slickness of the inner folds and Megan knew that her nubbin jutted high and taut.

Eyes closed, her mind drifted back to happier times when Zacora was first brought to the castle. She was very shy and so beautiful. A glorious heaviness settled upon Megan's breasts, making them swell against the black silk. Soon she slept. Gareth, satiated, was not far behind her.

Zacora lay on the filthy floor of the cottage. The bonds at her wrists and ankles were rubbing uncomfortably and she sighed.

"What's wrong?" she heard Callan whisper. "Are you in pain?" There was a pause, and she could feel him shuffling and trying to help her.

"I've made three recent mistakes in my life," she whispered, wishing his fingers would keep out of the way.

"What are they?"

She sighed again. He was deliciously handsome, but he was a slave and not the man she wanted to spend the rest of her life with.

"One was running away from the Meleagan castle." She listened to the soft sounds of sleep issuing from their three captors. "Then I thought perhaps the Prince was the man I wanted, but I was wrong."

"Well, you have me to look after you!"

"You were the third mistake," said Zacora sadly. "I'm ambitious and I'm noble." She could feel her wrists becoming free. "Take me to Harold the Pretender."

"But -"

"I wish to go with you, not with these two that impose upon him."

"But -"

"Come, while they sleep. There are three horses in the garden. Let us go." The Meleagan steeds were placidly silhouetted against the dawn sky.

Callan was unsure how to cope with this suddenly dominating young woman, who sounded so like Bernlada, his previous helpmate.

"And take this awful animal skin from me."

"But you'll be cold," he protested.

"Rather cold than smelling to high heaven." She stood still as he snipped the fur from her nakedness. She wriggled gratefully, delighting in regaining her freedom.

Callan looked longingly at her luscious body.

"Hurry!" she said impatiently, picking up the discarded ropes. "Into the garden."

Moving quietly they left the cottage, hearing the Meleagans grunt at the slight sound of disturbance. How she longed for Harold to realise her motives!

"Right," she said efficiently. "I want you to use these ropes to tie me to one of the horses."

Callan gasped at her disbelievingly. "Tie you to a horse?" he questioned at last.

"That's right." It was difficult for Zacora to hide her irritation. "Take me as a prisoner, for who knows who we may meet on the way? If soldiers, you may say you are returning me to the Prince." She was stammering with irritation. "Hurry up!" She waved a hand at the sleeping Meleagans. "They'll wake up any moment." Zacora took Callan's hand and led him to the low door.

It was wonderful to be out in the fresh air after the stale air of the tiny cottage. Callan stood a yard away from her, eyeing the mouth watering sight of her.

"Please, hurry," she said, her voice becoming softer and less dominant as she handed him the ropes. "Make sure that my hands are tied behind my back and I am facing the rear of the horse."

"The rear?" Callan sounded astonished.

"You must humiliate me as much as possible," she explained. "Put the rope between my buttocks, between my legs and around my neck."

Reluctantly, Callan did as she wished, placing her on Harold's huge stallion so that her legs were fully splayed. "Now tie my ankles, to spread my legs yet further," she ordered, "and lastly, use a piece of cloth to gag me."

Once she was settled in place, with her tumbled golden curls falling over her shoulders to caress her proud breasts, Callan reached up to stroke the soft slope of her fine belly, but she edged away, her eyes lowered humbly, again the passive embarrassed maid.

Callan, lithe and athletic, swung on to the big stallion, revelling in the feeling of the beautiful naked buttocks against his leather-clad body. The dual suns of Vakir, one in the east and one in the west, broke over the horizon together, bathing everything in rose and purple light.

Within minutes Zacora's precautions were justified. They met a young traveller who, after making pleasantries with Callan, insisted in trailing behind them, gazing up at Zacora in awe. "Are you taking her to the auction?" he wanted to know. "That isn't until the day after tomorrow."

"She's a runaway sex slave," said Callan sternly. "I'm returning her to her owner."

"I wish I owned her," said the young man, stroking the growing bulge in his tight hose. "She wouldn't run from me. I'd keep her busy."

"That's what they all say," said Callan, playing his part.

The young man looked increasingly uncomfortable. It was a very large bulge which was ascending in his tight hose, making his jerkin flare like a short skirt. "May I touch her?"

"Very well," agreed Callan. They stopped to allow the young man access. Zacora sat very still on the broad back of the horse, looking straight ahead while the young man gazed admiringly at her fully revealed sex.

An arm, clad in a torn home-spun shirt, reached up to the gaping moistness of Zacora's cunt. She was open to him, available, and the thought made her tremble. The emotion was not fear, but excitement, she knew. A stranger was reaching up to caress her pouting labias. The silver fronded lips seemed to arch out to him from the broad back of the horse.

"One moment, kind sir," the young man said in a hoarse, urgent voice. "I cannot reach the slave's beautiful nest, but I have a box in my pack which will aid me."

"Hurry then," said Callan impatiently. "The morning is well broken and we are anxious to be on our way."

The box placed in position, Zacora lowered her soft blue eyes to the young man and watched his fingers gently push the rope to the side. It had chafed her clitoris which rose to swollen, inflamed erection, the tip arched pertly. The young man gasped with delight and used a grubby finger to touch the heated little nubbin. Zacora felt her body flush at his touch. She knew she was wrong to have encouraged strangers to take such action, but it was the only way to return to the palace without Callan being severely punished.

The intrusive finger slid down to the delicate membrane of her entrance, feeling the silky wetness and the inviting portals. She shuddered as the finger penetrated deeply into her, driving in until the palm was pressed upon the downy cushion of her mound. The heel of the young hand, rough with hard work, grated on the hard projection of her nubbin. She could not help but move with him and soon she found her body arching back to take the full pleasure. The big horse twitched under her and she knew that her sex sap was wetting the big creature's smooth coat.

The young man slumped over the stallion's rump and Zacora knew that touching her, seeing her fully disclosed sex and feeling its reaction under his rough hand, had been too much for his male package. It had spilled its contents within his tight hose.

"We must go," said Callan. "Too much time wasted. We are chased by those who say they own this beauty."

It was full daylight with the suns warming the forest path. Zacora shook back her cascade of golden hair shot with silvery lights in the sunshine and pouted her full breasts to take the full benefit of the warmth of the suns.

The rough rope chafed the tender skin of her bottom cleft, irritating the membrane of her rear entrance. She wriggled, for the roughness made her remember the gnarled feeling of the young man's work roughened hands. It wasn't unpleasant, that memory.

Suddenly, Callan reined in. "Listen," he said, keeping the horse very still. At first all Zacora could hear was the gentle rustle of the breeze through the branches of the trees, but then another sound infiltrated into the noises of the forest. Hoofbeats, steady and moving fast.

Callan kicked his heels into the horse's flanks and the big beast moved off quickly. The rhythmic movement of the wide back under her was both stimulating and comforting. Her warm liquid oozed out of the open lips copiously and wetted her already excited clitoris.

The sound of hoofbeats, a group of horses, was much closer now. Zacora also heard the sound of laughter; very loud, male laughter. Men were talking as they rode.

"We've got to hide!" said Callan. "They're riding fast and they're very close now." His voice was low and breathless. "It will be the Prince's soldiers!"

Zacora, gagged by the piece of rag, was unable to comment. Callan reined in, looking round frantically. The forest was dense, but the horse was big, not an easy animal to hide, He jumped down, quickly untying Zacora's ankles and helping her dismount. In doing so, one hand brushed the softness of her downy thatch and felt the moist strands where the puffy lips parted. He raised his dark eyebrows, a knowing smile on his lips. His hands remained where they needed to be to lift her willowy form from the horse, his thumbs grazed the side swell of her full breasts, and his fingers slid to cup the warmth of those mounds. He heard her sigh behind the gag and she lowered her thick lashes.

He took this as an invitation and slid his hand over her belly, behind the rope which bound her wrists to her slender neck. His fingers slid down to cup the moist silver fronds, to part them and to enter the silky valley in which female treasures lay. She sighed again and her body flushed with heat as he touched the hardened love bud.

Her sapphire eyes gazed up at him. Her breasts were hard against his broad chest and she could feel her nipples become tender with their tension; the fine erectile skin gathered to hardened nubs. Her bound arms, the wrists chafed by the rough thick rope, caused her breasts to press closer to him. The spiky hemp rubbed roughly into the moist leaves of her sex, sensitised her nubbin, making it jut further from its hiding place. The rope caressed the plumpness of her mound, skimmed the slimness of her belly and up to her throat. Its tautness held her head bowed and, when she looked up, it cut cruelly into the wet skin of her sex leaves.

"Ah-ha! And what have we here?"

The gruff voice broke the spell between Zacora and Callan. They had been so engrossed with each other that they had not realised that they had been seen.

"A runaway perhaps?" It was the same voice. The speaker jumped down lithely from his horse and approached the two. He wore the uniform of a sergeant: light chain mail over a short leather jerkin. He rubbed the chain codpiece protecting his male package, grinning loudly.

"A beauty," he grunted. "A real beauty."

"She ran from the Palace - I am returning her." Callan's tone was firm and decisive. "No doubt there will be a reward."

"Is that right?" The sergeant tested the firmness of Zacora's bonds and nodded approvingly. "We shall escort you, then." His large hands tested the weight and softness of the breasts so tautly pressed out by the ropes binding her slim wrists. A finger grazed down the bond cutting through the valley of her breast flesh and down to the pouting silver mound.

Other men gathered round, watching the sergeant's actions avidly. He tugged on the rope, enjoying the way its roughness sliced into the drooling valley of the sex purse, parting the swelling lips and grating the bud of the clitoris. Without any thought of how the delicate skin of her cunt might be chafed, he pulled harder on the rope so that it pressed into the depth of her bottom flesh.

"She looks like the slave..." The sergeant hesitated, turning Zacora round to examine the peachy fullness of her buttocks, admiring how the binding dipped deep into the cleft. "The new slave that we have all heard tell of, the one Prince is so pleased about."

The gag was torn from Zacora's mouth, baring the very kissable lips. "It must be her!" said the sergeant gleefully. "There cannot be two such beauties! The reward will be large!"

There was laughter among the men, specially from one who had pushed to the front of the group and was eyeing Zacora avidly; her proud breasts, the soft blue eyes, the flowing golden hair and the always parted lips. In her bonds she looked so vulnerable and yet so willing as she flicked her gaze from one to the other of the men. "Who will know if we have borrowed a woman whose role is purely sexual?" said the bold one.

The sergeant nodded. "Aye," he agreed, "who will know?" he turned to Callan. "We'll bind this man, her protector, and deliver her ourselves. When we have finished with her. Fetch chains, ropes, anything."

"There is no need," Callan said huskily. "I shall not stop you, nor claim any reward, I will go my own way. But first I shall join you in whatever you wish to do to this woman." His penis throbbed at the thought of completing that which was thwarted at the cottage. It was erect and ready; already dewy on the globe. He stroked it slowly, grazing the tautness of the balls at each side of the peak of the shiny end.

"We'll leave her bound," said the sergeant, already removing the chain mail codpiece from his own throbbing erection. The other men drew around Zacora, grinning with anticipation.

There were ten men, including the sergeant. Each was in his prime; heavily muscled, tall and in peak condition. They all wore helmets with visors over the eyes, but their lower faces were free. They wore hose, in the fashion of the time. Knit in fine wool homespun, it showed off their superbly muscled legs and the heavy bundles of their masculinity to perfection. On active service, they wore armour in the form of chain mail which would make repulse but the sharpest swords. Preparing for entry into Zacora, they had bared their male weapons. All were rigid and throbbing.

Zacora, her arms still bound and the rope tightly holding her sex lips apart, looked up at the tall group of men, allowing her lips to curve in a sweet smile. There was a nervous tremor about the smile, for she had never been called upon to take so many men before. They were all so big. Their cockshafts were wide and long. She shuddered at the thought, but in her belly there was that excited swirling feeling of molten anticipation.

Callan pointed to a massive fallen oak. The trunk was as wide as the horse's back; the bark rough and gnarled. It rested on thick broken branches so that it did not lie flat, but slightly at an angle.

"If she was positioned correctly, that might be a useful addition to our needs," suggested Callan formally.

Hand resting slightly on the slippery silkiness of his globe, the sergeant looked at Zacora's lovely open face; at the luscious curves of her figure, at the way the rope disappeared so invitingly into the softness of her sex. "Yes," he agreed, "you could be right." He frowned as a thought crossed his mind so heavily involved in plundering the beautiful body. "Do we need to tie her?"

Callan shook his head. "She is quite pliant." His eyes narrowed, became darker as he gazed into Zacora's wide blue ones. "She desires to be violated and to pose for her plunderers."

Zacora knew that he was angry with her for being so bold, but it seemed to be in her nature. It wasn't what she chose to be. It was what she was.

"Ah-ha!" The sergeant nodding his head eagerly. "She is a born sex slave."

"So it would seem," said Callan softly. "But she can be tied if you wish?"

"If YOU wish. You seem more knowledgeable in these matters," said the sergeant. "What is your position in the palace?"

"Official Procurer of Potency to the Prince," Callan said, almost under his breath.

A sigh of admiration whispered through the small group and they watched carefully as Callan placed Zacora on her stomach, facing down the massive trunk. Her long legs were splayed around the rough bark. The rope was tight around her wrists and her head was pulled back as the truss disappeared into her clefts, front and rear. He placed a pillow of gathered moss under her belly so that the front and rear orifices would be available as he pulled the rope to the hollows between thigh and body.

"I loved you," he hissed in her ear as he made adjustments to her position.

"You are merely a slave."

"So are you!"

The sergeant and his men were becoming impatient. "What's going on there?"

Callan stood up, thrusting his penis forward as if to confirm his mastery of the situation. "A slight rebellion on the slave's part," he explained. "Nothing serious, I assure you."

"Fine," said the sergeant impatiently. "Let's get on with it. Since I am the most senior of the guards, I shall go first."

"She is capable of taking three men at a time," Callan said quickly.

Zacora gasped. Excitement with a tinge of fear made her slim belly flutter. She felt the cool softness of the mossy pillow under her hot skin and bore down into it, making sure that her moist pouch was fully open and her rear mouth was readily available. She could feel the roughness of the rope between her full breasts, and to this was added the grating of the old bark. This last seemed to make her nipples more tender, more sensitive, and her whole body more receptive.

"Three men at one time?" questioned the sergeant. A frown creased his face, handsome but weather beaten. "How so?"

"You will note," said Callan, "how I have forced her head up." He squatted down, his erect penis swaying before Zacora's eyes. She could see its eye moist, but not yet dripping. "If you, or one of your men, put legs wide and ease your cock into her mouth you will find it a wonderfully satisfying experience." He stroked Zacora's silky hair. She made no protest, but simply parted her lips in readiness.

The mens' eyes shone as the idea became clear. "And one of you can penetrate her in the usual way," added Callan. He parted and lifted the puffy labia and pushed fore and middle fingers into the socket, then held the glistening fingers up for all to see, and the men sighed in appreciation.

Zacora lay on the rough log, waiting. Callan was humiliating her deliberately, but she smiled softly to herself. Harold was the master, the master of humiliation, and soon, she hoped, she would belong to him.

"And lastly, one of you will penetrate her rear," Callan said softly. "It will be tight, and will require lubrication. This can be taken from here." The two fingers smeared into the parted softness once more and they were brought out gleaming and dripping. Callan massaged the pert rear tightness until Zacora could not help but grip the soft intrusion.

The eager soldiers understood how to take their pleasure quickly and were soon in position. Only one, that taking the female entrance, found difficulty in sliding under Zacora and slipping in his penis.

Two others, too impatient to wait their turn, stood over the sex slave's helpless form, slicking their fingers up and down their throbbing stems.

Callan stood by, one hand on his rigid manhood and one hand, at intervals, caressing Zacora. The pale oval of her face was stroked by the soft back of his hand, which sometimes strayed to the busy lips, stretched wide around the soldier's penis. Callan encouraged her wild sucking; encouraged the tongue which flickered tantalisingly over the man's leaking globe.

Occasionally, Callan's free hand took the flesh of a breast, kneading it hard so that Zacora found herself making murmurs of both pain and pleasure. He bent to suck the extended nipple, lapping at it wetly as he stroked his mound.

He listened to the sounds on the sensual forest path; the murmurs of sweet ecstasy, the sounds of wetness, bodies linked by the pleasure. Zacora reared as a powerful orgasm hit her, jerking her flesh with the voluptuousness which threshed through her.

It seemed to be a signal. The two men standing, their hands grasping their cocks like enormous fleshy weapons, grunted loudly, and Callan watched as they spumed hot creamy jets over the sex slave's body.

Zacora, her head held back by the rope around her long slim throat, began to swallow as the man spearing into her mouth spurted into it. There was a great deal, Callan could tell, from the way the girl was forced to swallow quickly.

The soldiers embedded deep inside Zacora were sweating profusely. The moisture ran in tiny streams down their ruddy faces. It was obvious that they were straining to hold back their pleasure; to prolong it. They rutted into her, pacing each other. One could feel the strength of the other's insertion through her delicate flesh, but the delight was too much and with a duet of hoarse growls they pulled from the syrupy nests to pool their issue on the already slicked skin of her back.

Zacora, head still arched back, looked up at the men. She may have been humiliated by these rough soldiers but the pride was still there on her lovely face. Callan fell upon her, unable to hold back his passion any longer. The other soldiers, those who had not taken her, took their turn. They were rough, grinding into her, scraping the tender skin of her belly on the bark.

Callan was roughest, screwing her ferociously and mouthing obscenities in her ears. His hands gripped the tangled mass of her golden hair and pounded his weapon deep inside her. She could feel the dark crisp curls of his pubis grinding against the fine flesh of her pouting buttocks and his roughness hurt; physically and mentally. He was punishing her for discarding him, but his roughness was exciting. A molten flood of pleasure swirled in her belly, sucking her down into it until she thought she would never surface.

CHAPTER SIXTEEN

"Well, now," came the familiar mocking voice of Harold the Pretender. "What a pretty sight!"

They had all been too intent upon their molesting of the captive to hear the approaching horses, which had come stealthily, not along the forest path but through the leaf strewn woodland.

As her assailants tried in vain to hide their shame, Zacora said nothing. But the moist sapphire eyes spoke volumes. 'Oh, I'm so pleased to see you, Harold. Look what he's made me do. Look how he's tied me and given me to these soldiers before taking me himself. He's a wicked cruel man and he was going to give me to that awful Prince. I want to be your slave. Just yours!' The words were not spoken, but her limpid, loving eyes and parted lips caressed the man who had bought her and was now about to save her.

"There, there, my sweet," he soothed, as if he heard her unspoken thoughts.

He turned to the guards. "This will not do!" he thundered. "I shall report this matter to the Prince! We shall go there now and I shall put him in place for good." He looked at her, resplendently naked and splayed upon the log. Her wrists were still bound and positioned at the very top of her buttock crease. His dark mature eyes, so full of knowledge and wisdom of the ways of young girls, took in every detail of the helpless body.

The delicate creamy skin of the curvaceous buttocks were marked from the rough handling they had received from the soldiers and Callan. Harold smoothed these marks, tracing them as if trying to remember them forever. He replaced the rope, dampened by the splashes of the soldiers' semen, into the depths of Zacora's buttock crease, making sure that it was still tight along the length from wrists to neck. His smooth and knowing hand slipped under her body to feel the silver downy softness of her pubic bush. He cupped it, delighting in the way the rope chafed the pouting flesh. With two fingers, splayed into a wide V, he felt the parted labia, admiring their plump firmness, so beautifully enhanced by the tightness of the rope.

Zacora lay still. She knew better that to move when Harold touched her. He enjoyed her body when she was still and passive, allowing him to investigate slowly and lovingly.

He parted the damp labia yet more, forcing the rough hemp of the rope into the soaking valley of her sex pouch. Zacora was unable to prevent herself jerking as the bond snapped on to her sensitive clitoris.

Harold's skilled fingers stroked the moist bud which reared for him. He lightly traced around the base of the perimeter of the shaft, feeling the silkiness of the lubrication. Inexorably, the finger teased. First it rubbed the erect top of the tiny shaft, staying well away from the sensitive tip. Zacora made mewing sounds but remained still, leaving the choice of his pace entirely to him. He felt the bud move under his touch, flutter engagingly like an insect preparing to break from the imprisoning chrysalis.

Zacora peeped over her shapely shoulder through tumbled locks, and he met her eyes, twinkling his dark knowing ones into the innocence of her blue orbs. The finger stroked each side of the silky shaft. She was breathing rapidly. Her bonded arms drew back as she tried to enhance the sensations being given by Harold, by stroking her erect nipples upon the rough bark of the old oak. She wanted her release. Her buttock muscles twitched involuntarily. If only he would raise her tiny hood, stroke the sensitive tip and be done with this teasing.

"Shall I whip these men?" Harold had almost forgotten that she and Gareth were with him until her harsh voice broke the spell. He released his hold on the damp valley of Zacora's sex purse and rose, holding the embroidered robe tightly closed to hide the stiffness and length of his erection.

Zacora, totally enslaved to her master, physically, mentally and emotionally, mewed piteously as he moved away from her body. She was ignored, for Harold must deal with his business before his pleasures.

"They must be punished," he said thoughtfully.

The soldiers, heads bowed, stood waiting to hear their fate. They knew that they could not expect mercy for the Meleagan family were well known for their discipline, even outright cruelty.

"I asked if I could whip them," said Megan testily. Gareth was watching, his slight body moving from foot to foot, his hands twitching around the growing bulge in his tight breeches. He loved to see the infliction of pain. It excited him, but he was unable to stand it upon himself.

A broad smile lit up Harold's face. "I have a plan," he said, "much more subtle than the sometimes inelegance of whipping."

Megan frowned. Gareth looked disappointed.

"Nevertheless," conceded Harold, pointing to Callan, "you, Megan, may remove that one's leather breeches and flay his buttocks most thoroughly."

Zacora felt a new flush of excitement make her body pinken prettily. He deserved it, she thought, treating her the way he did as Harold entered the forest clearing.

"But what of the guards?" Gareth wanted to know.

Harold smiled again; a secretive wicked smile. "Do we have spare rope or chains?" His eyes flickered across the men, standing so meekly awaiting their fate. One of them was sneaking a look at Zacora's still helpless body on the fallen oak. There was a tremor, a filling out, of the man's penis. Harold's eyes shone. It was exactly what he was expecting. "Well? Have we, or have we not?"

Gareth was eagerly searching through the pack on his horse. "We have both," he said, holding up a bundle of ropes and chains.

"Excellent!" commanded Harold. "As Megan attends to the palace servant, you, Gareth, will bind each of our guards about the penis so that there can be no movement. Do you understand?"

"Oh, yes!" said Gareth eagerly. "Oh, yes!" The slight figure bounced across the clearing and, Zacora, from the corner of her wide sapphire eyes, could see that the young man was grossly excited.

The soldiers were murmuring miserably. "Will this punishment be a permanent thing, master?" asked the sergeant.

"Certainly not," said Harold, quite hurt at this suggestion. "Do you take me for a cruel man?"

There were faint sighs of relief from the soldiers, but no-one answered Harold's question.

Megan busied herself tugging Callan's leather leggings from his beautifully muscled body, exclaiming as each muscle was fully revealed, delighting in the taut buttocks. "These will take the whip well," she murmured happily. She took him to a broad elm tree and, with some reluctance on his part, bonded his arms around the tree by tying his wrists about its girth. She spread his legs, delighting at his grunts of pain as she pressed his naked genitals to the trunk. His ankles were bound separately on each side of the sturdy elm.

Harold smiled at his assembled guard, watching them shudder at Callan's treatment. "I wonder how you will take your punishment," he said thoughtfully. "Let us see. Gareth, if you please."

The lad tested a fine chain for strength and resilience. The sergeant stepped forward, his head now held proudly upwards, ready for the treatment. He shuddered a little as the cold chain touched his naked flesh. It was wrapped around his slim groin, tying his penis tightly downwards. The chain was wrapped around the victim several times, cutting into the fine skin of his sperm sac and shaft.

With ropes and chains, each guard was treated in the same manner. Megan was flexing her whip, giving it a few peremptory flicks on the forest floor and delighting in the expressions on the faces of the guards and Callan, bound so tightly to the tall elm.

"What now?" Gareth wanted to know. "What would you wish me to do with them now?"

The same secretive smile creased Harold's handsome face. "Gags for all, I think," he said softly. The forest was hushed, waiting. Even the birds were silent, perched upon the branches looking down upon the scene. The leaves were still on the trees. Under the strength of the two suns of Vakir, the heat of mid-day was oppressive, the men, in their heavy chain mail, sweated. Moisture ran copiously, from heat and apprehension, down their faces and necks. "And, for safety's sake, bind their wrists behind the buttocks," added Harold after some thought. "We don't want them running amok."

It didn't take persuasion for Gareth to do his bidding.

Megan was frowning.

Harold turned to her. "You seem perplexed, my dear." He was slowly loosening his richly embroidered robe.

"It doesn't seem much of a punishment for the guards to be bound like that," she said testily. "They're frightened enough about being caught with your sex slave. Their weapons are very limp."

Harold slipped from his robe. He wore a richly jewelled codpiece. The precious stones caught the rays of the dual suns and the effect was dazzling. He stood legs apart, displaying the rich bundle proudly, like a strutting peacock about to fan out its tail.

The codpiece was well-filled, both between the muscular thighs and below the flat well-toned stomach. A dark band of hair bisected the flesh, giving the effect that the penis was already free from its jewelled pocket.

Zacora's sapphire eyes peered over her smooth shoulder in awe. The contents of the richly decorated package, she was sure, were for her. She was mesmerised by the sight. The other men in the forest clearing meant nothing to her.

The codpiece was held in position by jewelled bands and, so slowly as to be tortuous, Harold released these from his neat waist and from between his taut buttocks. His penis speared up, thick and gleaming, and Zacora caught her breath at the sight.

"For you, my dear," he whispered, striding over to her, with long easy strides. As if she was as light as a sack full of feathers, he lifted her from the fallen log. "This sword of mine is for you."

Zacora was aware that they were being watched. The guards, gagged and with their wrists bound, their shafts chained or roped to prevent erection, watched as she was laid upon a steep mossy bank. Her arms were still bound behind her, with the rope rising between her swollen flesh lips to her chafed neck.

The avid eyes of the guards never left her. They watched as Harold gently parted her long graceful thighs and positioned them so that the knees were loosely bent. Her buttocks were pressed up by her bound hands, giving the effect that her sex purse was offered high to Harold.

She knew that she was wet; that moisture gathered on the pink open-ness of her sex leaves. She knew that her clitoris was darkly inflamed, the hood drawn back. Most of all, she knew that her female entrance was pulsing beautifully for penetration.

Her breasts were swollen, tender. They, too, were offered to her master; willingly, gladly. He seemed to know and he bared his strong white teeth, grating them painfully over the erect buds.

From the corner of her eye she saw Callan watching. He had a look of longing on his dark features. The bonding to the tree seemed to excite him for his naked buttocks were pouting and his penis, closely bound though he was, was patently rigid and eager.

Megan was eyeing Zacora, her expression both spiteful and envious. The sex slave could not help wondering whether the envy was for her beauty or the attraction which Harold felt. His hands were dancing lightly over her inner thighs, spreading them so that there would be no hindrance when he finally penetrated her. Zacora placed her naked feet together, forming a circle of wanton-ness with her legs. This action had the effect of lifting her silver fronded mound, already raised closer to her adoring eyes by her bound hands at her buttocks. It also spread her moist leaves outwards, making it fully available to him.

Harold sighed and knelt at her side, his male flesh held tightly in his hand, testing its firmness.

"Are you ready, my sweet?"

"Always, for you, master," she whispered.

He knelt, like a supplicant, within the circle of her long legs, and swayed the heavy length of his shaft across her silver mound. The fullness of his balls nestled in her wet open sex pouch.

"Now!" she begged. "Now! Now! NOW!"

She looked up at him, the chafing of the rope reminding her of her slavery to him. His dark head was thrown back in ecstasy, completely ready to plunge into her, but he was so controlled and so completely the master, that he could restrain himself.

At last, he eased her legs to the fully open position. He delicately poised his swollen globe at her pulsing entrance and plunged inwards. Zacora sighed ecstatically at the deliciously full and fulfilled feeling.

Somewhere in the distance of her mind Zacora could hear the resounding crack of Megan's whip smacking naked flesh. It caused a great flood of sex sap to torrent over Harold's penetrating shaft. The excess oozed hotly over her lifted buttocks and over her bound hands. In spite of her slavery the excitement gave her emotional freedom and she arched gladly to her penetrator.

The crack of the whip came again, sharper this time, more cutting. Far away she thought she heard a groan of agony, muffled and gagged. It did not distract her, but simply heightened the delicious pleasure swirling in her belly. The swirl seemed to emanate from within herself, but also from the tip of Harold's cockshaft. With every plunge came the sound of the whip meeting bare flesh.

Other noises joined in the new symphony of the forest. There were muffled pleas, begging to be set free; groans of outright pain. Zacora looked to their source and saw the agony on the features of the guards. She could see, quite plainly, the chains and ropes cutting into the bulging flesh of cocks pinioned to prevent erection.

The broad chest of her master brushed lightly over the full swollen and arched mounds of her breasts each time he lifted his magnificent body to plunge into her. At each plunge she tautened her softness around his rigid flesh, caressing it and welcoming it in. He smiled down into her sapphire pools and seemed to sink into them, like a drowning man.

His plunges became more vibrant, more vigorous and she rose up to them. Her own surge took her by surprise. It seemed to lift her far above the dappled forest and, suddenly, he was with her. She felt him spurt hotly, again and again, until it seemed he would never stop. Her own climax seemed endless, shaking her from head to toe, time after time.

Zacora and Harold rested at last, satiated, satisfied, their goal achieved. Even Megan paused with the whip poised, and the soldiers began to experience a little relief.

Then, unexpected and intrusive, the voice of a girl dropped into the scene like a stone into a placid pond.

"What are you doing to Callan? That is my man." The voice rose as the words progressed, as though the owner was in a temper.

All heads turned towards her.

"Bernlada!" Callan had spat out his gag and was struggling against the tree and his bonds. "What are you doing here?"

Bernlada wore a short leather tunic, lightly tanned, so that it looked pale against her dark skin. Her small feet were shod in simple sandals held to her legs by long crossed thongs. Her dainty hands were strong and they soon wrenched the whip from Megan, who was taken by surprise.

"I know what you thought and you were wrong," said Bernlada sharply. "I was not going to leave you in the dungeons, my love. Anyway, everything went topsy-turvy after you left."

Megan, her plump breasts heaving in indignation, tried to prevent the newcomer from releasing Callan, but was repulsed very firmly.

"And who is this monstrous woman?" asked Bernlada disdainfully. She looked Megan up and down, taking in the clinging, far-too-short black silk dress and the all too evident red suspenders.

"Megan Meleagan," said Callan, rubbing his wrists and ankles. Not wishing to struggle into the tight leather breeches again, he cut a neat loin cloth and used it to cover himself, giving a heartfelt sigh of relief.

Bernlada smiled lovingly at him. "And who's that skinny fellow?" she wanted to know, pointing at Gareth.

"Another Meleagan," Callan informed her, taking her in his arms.

Bernlada turned to Harold. "Aren't you going to free those guards? The poor wretches look very uncomfortable."

Magnificently naked, Harold strode towards her. Even though he had emptied himself into the receptiveness of Zacora, he was still a sight to behold. "Yes, yes," he said impatiently, "but what of the Prince?"

"Ah yes." Bernlada paused. "Ah yes, the Prince. It was all too much for him. And besides his humiliation he knew the populace was against him, mobs had already been howling for his blood. He - he -"

"What?" asked Harold sternly. "What has that evil man done?"

"He - he - he knew he was finished -"

"Yes?"

"He fell upon his sword. He is dead."

"God be praised!" said Harold. "It is over then!" He looked back at Zacora's willing body. It was still open, ready for him, the legs splayed deliciously. The lovely face smiled sweetly, framed by the superb mass of tumbled hair, shimmering streaks of gold and silver in the light from the twin suns.

Surely she would bear him a son, a son worthy of the name Meleagan.

Bernlada's small body squared up to the big man. "What is all this to you?"

Tall, imperious and incredibly imposing, Harold beamed down at her, "No doubt the residents of the principality have had a thin time," he suggested, his muscular arms folded across his broad chest.

"Very," Bernlada agreed. "All the Prince could think of was producing an heir. Every drachma went on potions and spells to produce potency and nothing worked."

"I shall rule better, for I shall be at peace with myself." Harold glanced back at Zacora. She was so beautiful, so pliant, she would make a perfect consort. The combined lands of the Prince and the Meleagans would flourish and prosper under their care.

He turned to the guards. "The Prince is dead!" he said. "Will you follow me?"

A cheer went up.

"Come then. We will take the Palace." Chains were struck off and codpieces gratefully fitted in their rightful places. In his splendid robes and with Zacora sitting side-saddle in front of him, the procession prepared to move off.

"But what about us?" screeched Megan after them.

"Well, my dear," said Harold softly, "you seem to have carved out quite a steady little career for yourself. Please feel free to continue. Gareth can keep your accounts for you and you may use the castle as your work place. All the - er - equipment will be useful."

"And us?" Bernlada looked up at Harold beseechingly.

"Ah, yes." Harold gave the matter careful thought. "The cottage!" he exclaimed. "You may make it your home."

And at last there was sexual peace in Vakir.

Extracts

Erica, Property of Rex, *is one of the most popular Silver Moon titles. It begins like this:*

Paint was peeling from the woodwork of the dingy inner-city terrace house at the end of the pathetic strip of unkempt garden. The family might well have gone away after all that publicity: neighbours get very militant when youngsters are abused, even in this foulest of London slums.

The front door was ajar. I thought I heard crying from inside, or perhaps this was an abandoned kitten. Nobody answered my knock. The noise that had disturbed me stopped abruptly, that was all.

I pushed open the creaking door. It led to a bare narrow uncarpeted passage. In front I could see into a cheerless kitchen with unwashed dishes piled high in a sink with a dripping tap. A door was half open on my left. I went in, and there she was, lying naked on her stomach on a shabby green couch.

She turned over and sat up in alarm, an extremely pretty girl, obviously the one I was seeking, the one mentioned in those titillating press reports I had brooded over all this time. She tried to cover herself with the only protection she had, a very small cushion. For a moment big bewildered blue eyes peeped through long reddish-auburn hair which hung over her face in a haze, then she jumped to her feet and scampered to a corner as far away from me as she could get, turning to face me shyly, shaking her head so that the hair swung behind her. She was holding the cushion to her loins, but it could not conceal the fact that she had a perfect little figure, slim but nicely rounded. She stood very erect, which drew attention to those budding breasts, so high and firm.

There was no heating or comfort in that bare room, apparently no one else in the house.

"Are you Erica?" I asked.

"Yes." It was almost a whisper. She was shrinking into the corner. She had the wide sort of mouth that so easily shows the upper teeth, and hers were good, regular and very white.

"Where's your step-Mother?"

"G-gone to the pub."

"Does she always leave you like this, no clothes?"

"Oh no, but I mustn't go out because -"

"Because what?"

"Because, well you see, Uncle Willie is coming to - to punish me."

That troubled me, of course. In fact I had been troubled about 'Erica' ever since that first newspaper story - I have changed all names, for obvious reasons. As she cowered in the corner my eyes dwelt on her skin, so very smooth, a beautiful light brown, maybe olive, verging on golden, inviting the fingers to slide over it, all over it, to explore its shyness and secret recesses ...

I licked my lips. "I think I'll wait for your step-mother. Will she be long?"

"They'll be back any minute!"

"And your Uncle Willie is coming to punish you?" It seemed incredible. "What do you mean, punish?"

Extracts

She hesitated, biting her full lower lip. "He - he'll beat me, I think. With the belt, I expect, the leather one that hangs by my bed."

And here are a few paragraphs from Balikpan 1:

It was the cool of the evening on that first day of our trip. We hadn't even unpacked. We were strolling innocently back from a rather pleasant meal - consisting, it seemed, of rice and bits of highly spiced things floating in sauces - heading for our apartment block in Suriwong Road, still amazed by this culture where Sahdism is the official religion and women have no legal status other than as possessions.

We were more surprised than we should have been, therefore, to come upon a naked girl amongst the crowds, standing on a wooden box about eighteen inches high. Her wrists were strapped to her thighs, one on each side, and a stick with flags and balloons at the ends was jammed behind her shoulders, between upper arms and back, making quite a colourful display and thrusting her chest forward and her alluring bottom backwards.

Beside the girl, under the soft light of a street lamp, a man sat behind a trestle table set up on the pavement, a fly whisk in his hand. A selection of short thin gold and silver chains was lined up on the bare wood before him, each ending in a clip fashioned like a snake head.

Behind the man a medley of hooting traffic passed on the road, weaving in and out of the traffic lanes. Balikpan City late at night was like rush hour in London or New York, and passers-by still jostled for room on the pavement.

The girl on the box was evidently there to attract attention to these chains, for one linked her nipples by its two snake heads. For some reason I did not understand at the time, she was gagged. Apprehension sprang into her dark eyes as we stopped at the stall, and I saw her whole body, already covered in a thin sheen of perspiration, tense and start to tremble.

The man set aside the newspaper that had been spread before him, wiped his lips and set down his steaming cup, which must have come from the little cafe a couple of doors down the road: a few customers were inside, but most were eating at tables at the edge of the traffic.

Seeing our interest, the man heaved his weight to his feet, rubbing his hands and beaming at us.

He put down his fly whisk and held out a pair of clips. They would look great on Erica! If you pulled the chain both ends would close like jaws. "You buy?" he asked. He pointed to the selection laid out on his table. "Velly stlong bite. Me inwention, good, yes?"

He held one out for us to examine. The snake effect was very realistic, and Erica shrank back from it.

The man reached out and took hold of the chain linking the nipples of the girl on the box.

"See how how plitty? Not look stlong, yes?"

I saw the look in the girl's agonised eyes and realised why she needed to be gagged just before she landed sprawling amongst the feet of passers by...

Extracts

The Barbary Series of four titles is also extremely popular. This extract is from Barbary Slavemaster:-

"The woman I wish you to inspect," said the Pasha, "is said to be English and of aristocratic stock."

I was struck dumb by the thought of any English woman, let alone one of good family, being in the hands of a Marsa slave dealer. She would certainly be a rare and very valuable item!

"And you are also English and of good stock, Colonel Hussein," he continued.

"That is true," I said: I was still not used to being called Colonel Hussein of the Sultan of Turkey's Janissaries instead of Captain Rory Fitzgerald of His Majesty Kind George III's foot guards and the son of a penniless Anglo-Irish Baronet. The late Captain, owing to an unfortunate incident. "But now, of course," I hastened to add, "I am a true believer."

"May Allah be praised!"

"Indeed, Excellency," I murmured. I may as well admit, however, that my sudden conversion had been purely for practical reasons.

"My chief eunuch has of course examined this woman," the Pasha continued. "He says she is fit and well and can be trained satisfactorily."

I smiled at this. I knew well the impact such training would have on a white woman. Even in my own small hareem - one of the greater advantages of my religious conversion - the girls were kept very submissive.

"So," said the Pasha, "if the description is genuine I shall purchase her. Otherwise Ached shall suffer."

Achmet is a slave dealer, one of the more prominent in these parts.

[...we entered the display room...]

Here, there were Eastern carpets on the floor and bright painted tiles on the walls, but the windows were barred.

A shrinking figure stood upon a dais, hidden behind a loose white caftan buttoned down the front. Her head was covered in an all enveloping white veil.

"Speak to her," said the Pasha. "Speak to her in English."

He was getting increasingly impatient to get his hands on her. The chance of a well-bred English woman becoming a slave in Barbary must be remote indeed. However, it would be tactless indeed to disappoint the Pasha - specially when Achmet had bribed me not to do so on the way in, with the offer of another girl for my hareem.

The wrists of the woman on the dais were fastened behind her neck to a ring high up on the wall, thus keeping her upright and helpless to intervene when the buttons of her caftan were undone to allow the inspection of her body - she could then be freely seen and felt without interference.

The pose also bent her slightly backwards from the waist, which would raise her breasts and show them off to their best advantage, like the carved figure head at the prow of a ship.

Extracts

"Who are you?" I asked.

"Oh thank God!" The voice, though strained, was most attractive and definitely that of a educated young English lady!

Another author with four titles is Lia Anderssen with Biker's Girl I (extract below), Biker's Girl on the Run, The Training of Samantha, and The Hunted Aristocrat.

Lia felt the panic rising in her. "But you can't make me go in there like this!"

He smiled. "Like what?"

She lowered her eyes again. "You know."

He grinned, his eyes piercing hers. "You tell me," he said.

She hesitated. "I'm stark naked," she said quietly, blushing at having to say it.

"What?" he said, pretending to cup his ear.

Lia's face reddened more deeply. "I'm stark naked," she repeated, this time a little louder.

"I'm sorry," he grinned. "I just can't seem to hear you. Maybe it's the noise of the traffic. Perhaps you'd better tell me inside, and in a nice loud voice or I'll have to take my belt to you."

...The room was half full. At the tables sat men in dirty overalls, smoking and picking at grease-covered plates. In one corner sat another group of bikers...

Just beside her, on a pillar, was full-length mirror, placed there in better days to allow the clients to adjust their clothing before leaving.

She saw a slim, willowy figure, dark hair draped across her shoulders, the breasts not over large, but firm and jutting forward proudly, the dark nipples prominent and upturned, her belly dark with downy pubic hair kept trimmed short so that the lips of her sex were clearly visible, her long shapely legs tapering gracefullu beneath. She was probably the most beautiful woman that these louts would ever see cothed, let alone as she was.

She took heart from that as she opened her mouth...

And here are a few lines from 'Circus of Slaves' by Janey Jones-

Jasmine's inquisitive gaze froze and a gasp escaped her throat. She instantly became aware that a third person was present within the enveloping luxuriousness, and she stiffened like a surprised cat. In a dim corner there knelt, perfectly still, a small dark-haired female figure, head bent forward, legs spread, hands palm upwards on naked thighs, her wrists connected by fine silver chain. A helmet of shiny brown hair hung over her elfin face and her pale naked breasts shone like alabaster in the soft morning light.

Mr Columbus had turned and stood back, eyeing Jasmine closely from beneath his busy eyebrows.

"Let me introduce Tina, my personal assistant," he said.

All Silver Moon and Silver Mink titles available from shops £4.99 or (USA $ - varies) or direct (UK) £5.60 including postage or (USA) $6.95 + $2.95 per parcel

ISBN 1-897809-01-8 BARBARY SLAVEMASTER
ISBN 1-897809-02-6 ERICA:PROPERTY OF REX
ISBN 1-897809-99-9 BALIKPAN 1:ERICA ARRIVES*
ISBN 1-897809-03-4 BARBARY SLAVEGIRL
ISBN 1-897809-04-2 BIKER'S GIRL
ISBN 1-897809-05-0 BOUND FOR GOOD
ISBN 1-897809-07-7 THE TRAINING OF SAMANTHA
ISBN 1-897809-08-5 BARBARY PASHA
ISBN 1-897809-09-3 WHEN THE MASTER SPEAKS**
ISBN 1-897809-10-7 CIRCUS OF SLAVES
ISBN 1-897809-11-5 THE HUNTED ARISTOCRAT
ISBN 1-897809-13-1 AMELIA**
ISBN 1-897809-14-x BARBARY ENSLAVEMENT
ISBN 1-897809-15-8 THE DARKER SIDE**
ISBN 1-897809-16-6 RORIG'S DAWN
ISBN 1-897809-17-4 BIKER'S GIRL ON THE RUN
ISBN 1-897809-19-0 TRAINING OF ANNIE CORRAN**
ISBN 1-897809-20-4 SONIA**

*Direct only, £10 ($15)   **Silver Mink

Silver Moon Reader Services
PO Box CR25, Leeds LS7 3TN
or
PO Box 1614, New York NY 10156

FREE BOOKLET OF EXTRACTS ON REQUEST